"Forget the rules, ...ow your instincts."

Christine tilted her head to the side and opened her eyes. Travis was standing a kiss away from her. "What do your instincts tell you?" she asked.

"That I scared you because you don't know what's going to happen next. Well, I'll give you a hint. It includes you and me naked on this screened-in porch."

She gasped as the image flickered in her mind. It was daring and risky and...exciting.

She couldn't see Travis's expression. Was there a gleam of lust or triumph in his eyes? The porch was too dark, but she felt the tension in him. She grabbed the front of his shirt and pulled him forward. Travis went willingly and their mouths collided.

The kiss was hot and hungry. Anticipation swirled inside her. Christine slid her hands under his shirt, enjoying the solid muscle beneath her fingertips.

Travis's firm but gentle touch made her shiver as he undid the buttons on her blouse.

For once Christine didn't want to think about the future. She only wanted to focus on this moment.

And for tonight Travis was hers...

Susanna Carr has been an avid romance reader since she read her first Mills & Boon® Modern at the age of ten. Although romance novels were not allowed in her home, she always managed to sneak one in from the local library or from her twin sister's secret stash.

After attending college, and receiving a degree in English Literature, Susanna pursued a romance-writing career. She has written sexy contemporary romances for several publishers and her work has been honoured with awards for contemporary and sensual romance.

Susanna lives in the Pacific Northwest with her family. When she isn't writing she enjoys reading romance and connecting with readers online. Visit her website at: www.susannacarr.com

WILD WEEKEND

BY
SUSANNA CARR

Published in Great Britain 2014
by Mills & Boon, an imprint of Harlequin (UK) Limited,
Eton House, 18-24 Paradise Road, Richmond, Surrey, TW9 1SR

© 2014 Jasmine Communications, LLC

ISBN: 978-0-263-90928-9

Harlequin (UK) Limited's policy is to use papers that are natural,
renewable and recyclable products and made from wood grown in
sustainable forests. The logging and manufacturing processes conform
to the legal environmental regulations of the country of origin.

Printed and bound in Spain
by Blackprint CPI, Barcelona

WILD WEEKEND

Many thanks to my editor, Kathryn Lye

CHAPTER ONE

NEON LIGHTS FLICKERED inside the dark casino. The cold air was thick with cigarette smoke and the scent of sugary cocktails. Frank Sinatra blared from the loudspeakers.

So this is what hell looks like. Travis Cain automatically surveyed the room, although any sudden movement from the patrons was unlikely. Most of them were slumped in front of tables and slot machines, their expressions glazed over as they waited for something—anything—to happen. "There are other things I could be doing right now," he muttered.

"True." His friend Aaron nodded as he drank a fruity cocktail. "But how often do you get a chance to make money just by sitting around?"

Aaron made it sound so easy, but Travis was never good at sitting still. "Do you know what I could be doing right now? Wingsuit-flying over the Eiger."

"As if you had enough cash to fly to Switzerland," Aaron said as he motioned the blackjack dealer to hit him with another card.

"Surfing the big waves in Tasmania." Travis smiled as he thought about the crystal-blue water.

"You've already done that." Aaron sighed when he lost the hand. "You never repeat yourself."

"I saw something about bungee jumping." He'd jumped before, so it wasn't that much of a challenge, but it was better than staying in the casino.

"Dude, this is Las Vegas. Why would you want to do that

when everything you need comes directly to you? Entertainment," he said as he placed another bet. "Cheap drinks. Spa services."

The spa? Was he serious? Travis cast a glance at his friend's hand and belatedly noticed the manicured fingers. He looked at Aaron with horror, noticing everything from his long blond hair and groomed beard. Aaron's hands used to be caked in mud from digging up treasures. Now he was getting manicures? "What happened to you? Don't you crave adventure?"

"I started craving comfort. It happened the moment we kayaked that waterfall." Aaron closed his eyes and shuddered as he remembered that moment. "That was stupid."

It was a miracle that they had survived. "You've gotten old. Cautious." Travis made a face. "Married."

"My priorities have changed and I decided what I really wanted in life," Aaron corrected. "My dreams are bigger."

Bigger? Travis wanted to scoff at that statement. His friend's dreams had become *safer*. He now focused all his reckless energy on gambling. Unfortunately, Aaron turned out to be good at it.

"Wait until you get married," Aaron said as he motioned for the blackjack dealer to give him another card, "and then you'll know what I mean."

"Never going to happen," Travis said gruffly. Women only wanted one thing from him: a good story to tell their friends back home. He was the rebound sex or the vacation fling. Not that he had a problem with that.

Only the brave ones tried to make the affair go longer. He'd had a few serious relationships in the past and tried living in one place with one woman. Turned out he was horrible at it. No big surprise there.

His exes quickly realized he couldn't be domesticated. He did try. They wanted him to bring excitement and adventure to their daily schedule, but at the same time they didn't wel-

come chaos in their lives. His boundless energy was no longer attractive and his need to explore became less inspiring
and more exasperating.

"Travis?" Aaron lightly punched him in the arm. "Are you
listening to me?"

He hated sitting still. It gave you too much time to think
about mistakes and regrets. Limitations and personal flaws.
"No, but let me guess. You don't trust hotel security."

"After what happened in Rio? Hell, no," Aaron said with
feeling. "The thieves tore up my room and almost got the emerald. Good thing I had it on me that night."

That was the problem with all his friends settling down,
Travis thought as he took a drink from his beer bottle. He
may be envious that they'd found someone to share their lives
with, but settling down meant embracing the sameness. Same
conversations. Same retelling of their adventures. His friends
were content with that, but he wanted more stories to tell.

It was only a matter of time before Aaron launched into the
story about the emerald that was tucked in Travis's pocket.
How he won it from an unscrupulous guy named Hoffmann
in a game three years ago. Aaron had already reminisced
about that moment when he called Travis for backup. Aaron
was in Las Vegas on a poker-playing circuit with Hoffmann
and some high rollers and he was using the emerald again as
collateral. Unfortunately, the other players were not known
to be law-abiding.

"And yet you still want to play poker with these guys,"
Travis muttered. "If breaking and entering is part of their
routine, something tells me cheating is going to be second
nature to them."

"There is no evidence that Hoffmann or anyone from the
circuit was behind it."

"Right," Travis said sarcastically. "It's only coincidental
that a break-in happens when you enter a high-stakes poker
game with these guys."

"The only time that emerald is out of the vault is *when* I enter a high-stakes poker game. That emerald you're keeping safe in your jacket is my collateral."

"And your lucky charm," Travis added. His friend's superstitious nature brought them more problems than protection.

"That, too." Aaron leaned back in his chair and had a faraway look in his eyes. "If I didn't have that when we were chased out of that village on the Amazon River…"

Travis rolled his eyes. Why did his friend give all the credit to a rock? "I still would have saved you."

"Yes, but would I still have all my limbs? We'll never know." Aaron straightened in his chair. "Anyway, I've had that emerald with me whenever it counted. I had it when I met Dana."

"Had it when you married her," Travis finished for his friend. "I'm surprised you didn't add it to her engagement ring."

"She said emerald engagement rings are bad luck."

"Can't have that."

"Damn straight. But when I win this poker game, I'm going to buy her something nice. I saw this necklace in the window—"

Travis raised his beer bottle to his lips and paused when he saw a woman walk into the casino from the hotel lobby. She stood out from the crowd of T-shirts and jeans, wearing a skintight blue dress and platform heels. His gaze traveled lazily down her body. Travis did a double take when he saw what was in her hand. Instead of a designer purse or a weekend bag, she held a vintage mountaineering backpack. Only this backpack had never been used.

He slowly lowered his beer onto the table as his curiosity deepened. Travis glanced at her face and his heart gave a violent kick. She was a natural beauty. She didn't need to highlight her wide brown eyes or her full pink lips with a heavy layer of makeup.

The woman reached up and flipped her hair back. The movement pulled at her dress, emphasizing her gentle curves and athletic build. His gut clenched when he saw her long, bare legs. He'd bet they were silky smooth. Warm and strong. He wondered what those legs would feel like wrapped tightly around him. Travis gritted his teeth as his imagination bloomed.

"She's out of your league," Aaron said.

It was true, but that didn't make Travis ignore the woman. "Dana is out of your league, and look what happened there," he said gruffly.

"Dana is different. That woman? High maintenance. I see that kind of woman all the time in the casinos. Do you see how she's dressed? How she isn't with anyone? She's on the hunt for a big spender."

Travis shook his head as he watched the woman walk past a row of slot machines. She was a breath of fresh air in a kitschy casino filled with gold furniture and red carpeting. She was looking around, taking in everything. He had recognized the look in her eyes. She was ready for anything. "No, she wants excitement."

But what kind? The backpack indicated she wanted adventure but it didn't seem a natural fit. Her do-me-right-now shoes suggested she was looking for a good time, but she tugged at her dress as if she wasn't comfortable with the short length.

"She wants a glamorous lifestyle," Aaron corrected. "Financial security. Two things you don't possess."

"I'm getting big bucks to babysit the emerald," he reminded his friend. He would have done it for free to help out but Aaron had insisted. It was the only reason Travis would visit a place like Vegas.

"Which you plan to spend on climbing the volcanoes in Indonesia. Waste of money, if you ask me."

Travis reluctantly dragged his gaze away from the woman.

"You're just saying that because you want to come along. Dana won't let you, will she?"

"Hey, she worries about me," Aaron said with a smile. "And I kind of like that."

Travis frowned. It had been a long time since someone had worried about him. He used to prefer it that way. After being raised by his grandmother, who saw danger in every corner, he didn't want to be held back because of someone's fears. But the idea of a loved one caring about him didn't sound as suffocating as it should.

"You know," Aaron continued, "if you stopped spending your money on adventures and started investing it, you could have a very comfortable lifestyle."

There was that word again. *Comfortable.* The idea of comfort was a trap. If you're comfortable, you're too scared to take a risk. You're too busy protecting what you have instead of going for something you want.

"You could even have a chance with a woman like that."

"I could get her now," Travis declared, ignoring Aaron's bark of laughter as he looked for the brunette in the shadowy casino. He jerked his attention back to two men sitting next to the slot machines. They hadn't been there before. He noticed only one of the guys was playing. The tall one sat silently, his attention directly on the blackjack table. Their dark suits didn't hide their bulky physiques.

"Aaron, do you see the two guys at the slot machines?" Travis asked as he made brief eye contact with the pale guy with blue eyes. "Something's off. They're positioned to look directly at us. How much do you want to bet they are looking for the emerald?"

Aaron took a long sip of his drink as he casually glanced over at the slot machines. "You're being paranoid."

"Do they look familiar?" Travis asked as his instincts started tingling. "Did you see them when the thieves tore up your hotel room in Rio? They may have blended in with the crowd, but they don't fit in with this clientele."

"Neither do we," Aaron pointed out as he set down his glass.

"Exactly." The players for the high-stakes poker game purposely chose a cheap and shabby casino for privacy and secrecy.

"Those guys are part of Hoffmann's security team," Aaron said.

"How rich are these poker buddies that they need security?"

"Very. Although I think *security team* is another way of saying *enforcers*."

"Terrific."

"I think the one with the crooked nose is Pitts. The tall one is Underwood."

"You really need to learn the definition of *buddy*," Travis asserted. "A buddy does not put you under surveillance. I think you are being watched."

"You mean *we* are being watched," Aaron corrected.

"Do you think these guys are working for their boss or for themselves?"

Aaron frowned. "Hoffmann has been trying to win back the emerald. He says it's a family heirloom. He's getting a little desperate and he's had an unlucky streak."

"So if he can't win it back, his security guys are going to find it while you're in the game."

"We're making it too obvious that we're friends," Aaron said. "If they tear up my room and don't find the emerald, they'll search your room."

"Why me? You're the one who owns the gem."

"Process of elimination. If I don't have it on me or in my room, they will go after my closest buddy."

"Time to split up," Travis muttered. "Text me when you need me."

"They'll go after you," Aaron predicted. "You need to throw them off. How will you do that? You're a single guy who doesn't gamble. A lot goes on in Vegas, but you'll stick out like a sore thumb. You need to look less suspicious."

It was true. He needed to blend in with a group. Unfortunately, most of the guests in this place were senior citizens. He could infiltrate a bachelor party. Find a group of businessmen here for a convention. Travis looked around and his gaze landed on the brunette in the blue dress.

An idea formed in his mind. Travis rose from his seat, his pulse quickening with anticipation. Forget a bunch of drunk, rowdy men. He knew exactly how he wanted to spend his weekend. "I'll be with the brunette."

His friend snorted at the claim. "Her? Never going to happen."

"How can you say that? I'm holding on to your emerald," Travis replied. The emerald suddenly felt heavy in the breast pocket of his jacket.

Aaron laughed. "That emerald is lucky, not magic. But you'll find out soon enough."

SHE WOULD NEVER listen to Jill again, Christine Pearson thought as she tugged at the hem of her dress. Her friend insisted on this fancy outfit, telling her she would blend in with the crowd. Did Jill think she was staying at the Bellagio or something?

Christine took a step forward and felt her skirt rise up her thigh. She tried to yank it down as she walked, but she wasn't used to wearing high heels. She turned her ankle and almost tripped.

I should have stayed home. That had been the thought running through her mind the moment she got off the plane at McCarran Airport. She had headed straight for the restroom, found an empty stall and struggled into her tight dress and high heels.

The moment she had stepped out of the stall and seen her reflection in the mirror she knew the plan wasn't going to work. She wasn't the kind of woman to wear this dress. It was no use pretending. At least no one back in Cedar Valley would see her make a fool of herself.

Christine closed her eyes, but the chimes and bells from the machines were distracting. She took a deep breath only to inhale the stench of smoke. *You're here. Might as well make the most of this weekend.*

She opened her eyes and blinked as the bright lights flickered in the dark casino. It was time to focus. Flipping her hair back, Christine tried to remember her to-do list.

She sighed and rolled her eyes in self-disgust. That should have been her first clue that this plan wasn't going to work. Who made a to-do list for a wild weekend?

Her thoughts only proved that somehow, somewhere, she had lost her impetuous spirit. She hadn't realized it until she discovered the list of dreams she had written when she had turned eighteen. She really wished she hadn't found it. Every naive, ridiculous and impractical goal was on that list.

And yet, ten years later, she hadn't accomplished any of them. *Not one.* The regret weighed heavily on her. Where had all the time gone? What had she been doing? She marched across the casino floor. Was it possible that she had changed so much in ten years? Was she a completely different person now?

Christine stumbled to a halt in the middle of the casino as she considered that question. Was it too late to follow this list? Should she let it go and move on?

No. Christine raised her chin and rolled back her shoulders. If she were a different person, it wouldn't have hurt so much to see that list. She would have laughed it off and thrown it away.

Instead, she'd memorized it and decided to take action. It was time to resurrect her wild side and become the bold

woman she'd always wanted to be. She was starting it all off
with a three-day weekend in Las Vegas so she could have the
freedom to try something daring.

She walked by a row of old-fashioned slot machines and
paused. Fishing through her backpack, Christine pulled out
a crisp dollar bill and fed it through the machine. She pulled
the lever, but didn't feel any excitement as she watched the
row of symbols spin and settle.

She lost.

No surprise there. But that was dream number forty-three.
Win money. She knew why she had written that down ten
years ago. Back then she had big dreams and a poorly paid
summer position at the bank.

Now she was the manager of that bank.

Christine's shoulders slumped. That hadn't been the plan.
The plan had been to get out of Cedar Valley and find her
passion. She'd failed on both counts. Worse, she had a pristine dream list with nothing checked off.

Her eighteen-year-old self would be horrified.

Her twenty-eight-year-old self wasn't that impressed, either.

But she was changing that. All she had to do was check off
one thing. She could do that in Vegas, where no one would
judge her or rein her in.

Christine sat down next to the slot machine as she considered her list. What about number nineteen? *Climb Mount
Rainier.* Yeah, that's in Washington state and she was in
Nevada. Perhaps number eight? *Get a tattoo.* No. Christine
immediately discarded that idea. It was too permanent. She
needed to take a baby step.

Christine reached into her backpack for another dollar. She
saw a movement from the corner of her eye and looked up to
see a man stride down the aisle of slot machines.

Wow. Christine's eyes widened. The man was tall and lean.
She was mesmerized by the confident and smooth way he

moved. Her gaze went from his scuffed boots and his power-ful legs encased in low-riding, faded jeans. She noticed how his dark jacket hung from his broad shoulders and the way his white-collared shirt stretched against his muscular chest.

Christine glanced up and found herself staring. The man did little to control his dark wavy hair and her hands itched to sink into the softness. And then she would trail her fingers along his high cheekbones and angular jaw. She wanted to trace the grooves that bracketed his firm mouth and the lines that fanned from his sparkling brown eyes.

The man flashed a lopsided smile and Christine's breath hitched in her throat. Excitement bubbled inside her, heat-ing her body and pressing against her skin, ready to burst.

Christine slowly looked over her shoulder, wondering if he was smiling at a pretty waitress or an exotic dancer. No one was behind her.

She frowned and turned around. The handsome stranger stood in front of her. His smile was brighter, a slash of white against his golden-brown skin. He was so tall that she had to tilt her head back to look into his eyes.

"You have so many games to choose from and you try the slot machines?" The man's husky voice sent a thrill down her spine. "Where's the challenge in that?"

Why did that sound like a metaphor of her life? Christine cautiously returned his smile. "It doesn't require any skill."

"It's also the simplest way to lose money." He leaned against the machine. "The odds aren't in your favor."

"That doesn't surprise me." She nervously shifted in her seat and felt the short hem inch up. "I don't think the casino will offer a sure thing."

"Depends on what you're looking for."

Christine saw the gleam of interest in his eyes. She dragged air into her lungs as her skin felt tight and flushed.

No, no, no. She shouldn't entertain this idea. He was just chatting with her. He wasn't flirting. He wasn't suggesting he was a sure thing. That was just wishful thinking on her part.

Anyway, hot sex was not on her list. There was no mention of a fling or a one-night stand.

But that didn't stop her from allowing her gaze to drift down his body. There should be something about sex on her dream list, she thought as she bit down on her bottom lip. Something impossibly wild. A fantasy that would rock her world.

In fact, there was no reason why she couldn't add this sexy stranger to the list.

"I'm Christine." She held out her hand and belatedly realized her formal manner.

He wrapped his large, calloused hand around hers. He was big. Strong and masculine. She hoped he didn't feel the fluttering pulse at her wrist.

"Travis."

Hello, Travis. Otherwise known as number one hundred and one: have a weekend fling.

She froze as the words tumbled in her mind. *One hundred and one.* This was a mistake. How could she add him to the list when she hadn't crossed anything off? Was she trying to sabotage her goals the moment her vacation started?

Christine reluctantly withdrew her hand from his grasp. She immediately missed the warm, masculine touch, but she tightly folded her hands on her lap.

She wasn't going to get distracted from her dream list. Especially not with a man. She couldn't let that happen again.

CHAPTER TWO

TRAVIS WAS SURPRISED at Christine's withdrawal. One moment he saw the glow in her eyes and the next moment she'd banked it. It was as if she took one look at him and decided pursuing him wasn't a good idea. That *he* wasn't a good idea.

It wasn't the first time for him. Good girls and proper ladies kept their distance…unless they were looking for a good time. He was a momentary lapse of judgment or a vacation from real life.

He felt a twinge of disappointment that Christine wasn't going to act on the instant attraction. He liked the way she'd looked at him. It was a mix of excitement and trepidation. Anticipation and doubt. He knew that feeling—it was what he experienced every time he was about to embark on a great adventure.

He liked the idea of being someone's great adventure, and he wanted to see that wicked glow in her eyes again. Hold on to the promise of something special. It had nothing to do with his goal to blend in and everything to do with exploring the wild streak he saw inside her.

Travis knew he would have to be careful in his pursuit. He realized now that Christine wasn't as bold as she appeared. Despite the sexy dress that hugged her curves and the thirst for adventure in her serious brown eyes, this woman was quiet and reserved.

He should have picked up on that in the way she checked out the casino when she first stepped inside, but he wasn't used to hesitant women. This one observed before she moved forward. She didn't run headfirst into a situation, nor did she see an opportunity and grab it.

This was a woman who considered the pros and cons. She saw potential problems before she saw possibilities. He remembered how his grandmother used to do that and he always pushed himself to do the opposite. His mind-set worked because most people he met on his travels were impulsive, ready to forget common sense in their quest to go crazy before they had to return to their real life.

"What brings you to Vegas?" Travis asked. She was playing the slot machines with a decided lack of interest but was perched on the gold seat as if she were waiting for something wonderful to happen.

Christine was an intriguing puzzle. He felt the buzz of interest in his veins. Normally he felt like this right before he stepped into uncharted territory. But those times he knew the payoff would be big. Christine wasn't a sure thing but she was the challenge he was looking for in Vegas.

She tilted her head and gave him a quizzical look. "What makes you think I'm not from around here?"

Where should he start? Her attire was wrong for a casino and a Las Vegas native would know that. She was dressed more for a nightclub. He could also tell that the desert sun never touched her pale skin. Travis curled his fingers as he imagined she would be smooth and silky to the touch.

There was also the fact that she was dragging around a bag that had an airline sticker on it. He gave a casual shrug. "Just a wild guess."

"Do you live here?" she asked as she gave him a longer, more thorough look. "Is that how you can tell?"

"No, I don't have a home base." After feeling trapped in his childhood home, he chose not to have a permanent address these days. In the past few months he had lived everywhere from a hut in Belize to a pickup truck along Route 66.

He made good money along the way. Once he picked up a skill, he turned around and taught them to tourists. He could do anything from teaching people how to surf to guiding them through the jungle. "I don't really see the need for one."

"I don't think I follow," Christine said as her eyes widened. "You just pick up and leave whenever you feel like it?"

He nodded as he watched Christine's eyes cloud over. She obviously couldn't comprehend that kind of freedom, but he couldn't tell if she was envious or horrified. "I don't mind roughing it," he added. "Comfort and excitement don't go hand in hand."

She dipped her head and her long hair fell over her face like a veil. "You're right, they don't."

Christine's voice had been so quiet he almost didn't hear her above the ringing bells and shouts of laughter in the casino. Yet he caught the regret in her tone.

She straightened her shoulders and lifted her chin. "Once you have a comfort zone, it doesn't grow wider," Christine said as she tucked her hair behind her ear. "It gets smaller and smaller until you realize you've put yourself in a cage."

"Exactly," Travis slowly agreed. It was why he didn't stay in one place for more than a month. There were moments when he longed to call a place his own, but he'd grit his teeth and keep moving until the feeling passed. "Sometimes you need to shake things up. The way you're doing now."

"You can tell that just by looking at me?" She glanced at her dress and automatically pulled at the short hem that revealed her long, slender legs. "What else can you tell?"

Travis paused. He was usually good at figuring out people; the skill helped him survive whenever he found himself in sticky situations. But he got the feeling that Christine was trying to be someone different during her Vegas trip. He saw that a lot in the more touristy areas he'd visited. It was like role-playing, trying on a more exciting or an entirely different persona.

"This is your first time in Vegas," he guessed.

Christine jerked her head back in surprise. "That's true," she reluctantly admitted. She glanced around the casino as if she wondered how he'd come to that conclusion.

"First trip anywhere?" he asked.

"Not at all," she scoffed. She rubbed her fingers over her bare collarbone. Her hand stilled as if she realized something was missing. "I travel around the world all the time."

Travis silently nodded his head. It may not be the first time she'd been out of her hometown, but it was definitely the far-thest she'd been away from home. Only she didn't want him to know that. Christine wanted to look more sophisticated and experienced than she really was. How far was she willing to go to live out this role? Travis was willing to play along.

"I'm taking advantage of a long weekend," she said with a defiant thrust of her chin, "and I decided to try something closer to home."

He didn't buy that excuse. Christine was definitely the kind of person who would make incremental goals. Once she found success, she would build up to a bigger goal. He couldn't imagine living like that.

"What do you do?" he asked. It was probably a desk job that dealt with numbers. She would want something that was climate-controlled and dealt with absolutes. But what would her alter ego say? Would she pick something creative or some-thing dangerous? What she decided would give him a little more insight into her dream life.

Christine pursed her lips. "What do you think I do?"

Travis arched an eyebrow. It was time to rattle her cage. He reached out and grabbed her hand.

"Are you going to tell me my fortune?" Christine asked with a nervous laugh.

"No, but I can tell a lot about a person by their hands." Hers were soft and delicate. The nails were short and unvarnished. There was no wedding ring and no indication that there had been one.

"I can't tell what you do for a living," he said as he trailed a fingertip down her palm before resting it against her wrist. Her pulse skipped under his touch. "You are searching for a challenge. You've done it all. Seen it all."

Her hand jerked but she didn't pull away. "Go on."

"You're looking for a jump start."

She snatched her hand back. "What makes you think that?"

He wasn't sure why he said it. A jump start suggested she had once been adventurous but now found herself in a routine. That didn't sound right. She was too cautious. She wanted to be reckless but just couldn't let herself go.

"It's been a while since you had an adrenaline rush," he continued, watching her closely. He needed to see her response or have her correct him, but Christine's expression didn't give anything away. "Vegas may be too tame for you."

The corner of her mouth twitched as she leaned back in the gold seat. "Are you talking about me or yourself?"

"Can you read people, too?" he teased.

"No, but I looked around this casino when I came in," she said. She did a quick survey and looked back at him. "We don't fit into this crowd, so I have to wonder why you're here. The only other guy who's around thirty is the blond guy with a beard at the blackjack table. Are you with him?"

Travis froze. He hadn't expected Christine to be that observant. How had she already connected him with Aaron? Had she seen him talking to his friend or was there a detail he had missed?

"That guy?" He casually glanced over at where his friend was sitting. His gut clenched when he noticed Underwood and Pitts talking to Aaron. "Never met him before. I was giving him blackjack tips, but he didn't need them."

Aaron and Pitts looked over at him. Travis knew that wasn't a good sign and refused to make eye contact with his friend. He needed to distance himself from Aaron before they realized he was the one who had the emerald.

He didn't know why he assumed Pitts and Underwood wanted to steal the emerald. He just knew. Maybe it had to do with the instincts he had developed over the years. Or it could be because those two were around the last time someone tried to take Aaron's gem.

That emerald was bigger than any gem he and Aaron found on their treasure hunts. Any of his poker compatriots could be after it, but Hoffmann had more of an emotional investment in it since it was a family heirloom.

"Why are you in this casino, Travis?" she asked. "Do you work here?"

The idea of working hours in a dark and windowless room sounded like torture. Travis shuddered at the thought. He hated being indoors. It reminded him too much of home. "No, I'm here looking for business."

Christine gave a skeptical look. "You're a businessman?"

Travis shook his head. No one would believe that. He realized he should have planned a cover story so he didn't get caught in a lie. But why should he start thinking ahead now? He always thought on his feet. Not knowing what he was going to say or how he was going to get out of trouble was half the fun. "Most of these guys are senior citizens who like to gamble and invest in expeditions."

She blinked and it was as if the light went out in her eyes. "I see."

He knew that look. He got it all the time when he tried to fund his next extreme adventure. "I'm not a con artist or a grifter," he insisted, flattening his hand against his heart as if he was making a pledge. "I plan and guide friends through adventures."

"Yes, I can imagine there's a huge difference."

"I'm trying to raise money for my next trip," he added. He wasn't sure why he felt the need to tell Christine. He wanted

her to open up, but it felt as if he was the one who was telling
her everything. "I want to climb the volcanoes of Indonesia."

"Never been there," she said coolly. "But then, if you climb
one volcano, you've climbed them all."

Travis pressed his lips together. No climber would make
that kind of declaration. "Yes, I can tell you're an experienced
mountaineer with that backpack."

She reached down and touched the pack, as if making sure
it was still there. "I take it with me everywhere."

"It's in great condition for a world traveler," he commented
as he leaned more comfortably against the slot machine. "So
where have you been?"

She hesitated. "Everywhere but here."

"Hmm..." She wasn't giving him any information. He
needed a new tactic. Travis didn't think she was trying to be
mysterious. Was she worried she'd get caught in a lie or was
she out of practice talking about herself? "How long did you
say you're staying in Las Vegas?"

"Just for the weekend."

He could do a lot in Vegas in forty-eight hours. Take Underwood and Pitts on a wild-goose chase. All he needed was
a woman at his side who was game for anything. "Christine,
it sounds like you need a guide," he said with a smile. "I'm
happy to be at your service."

OH... CHRISTINE FOUGHT to keep a mildly interested look on
her face as disappointment washed over her. So that was what
this was all about. Her pulse had fluttered when she realized
Travis had crossed the casino floor to meet her. Her heart had
thumped against her ribs when she met his piercing brown
eyes. She felt like the exciting and fascinating woman she'd
always wanted to be.

It had only taken a moment to believe in the fantasy. But
Travis set her straight. He wasn't flirting with her. He wasn't
interested in her as a woman. Travis had given her his full

attention because that was his routine. He didn't want to bed her; he wanted her money.

Not even as a gigolo. No, her luck never worked like that. He wanted to be her tour guide.

She should have known. If she wasn't exciting enough for her ex-boyfriend, Darrell, then she really wasn't going to be spellbinding for a guy like Travis. Darrell was the most eligible bachelor in Cedar Valley, but honestly, there wasn't that much competition.

Travis, however, was different. He was so handsome that it almost hurt to look at him. He walked with the confidence of a man who had faced life-and-death situations. His hooded eyes couldn't hide the shadows or the hard-earned experience. Women were immediately drawn to a man like Travis. He was danger, fantasy and sex wrapped in raw masculinity.

He could have his pick of women. Travis probably had met thousands of women just like her. She had nothing new to offer him, nothing to hold his attention, except for her money. He should have picked someone richer.

"You're a guide?" she said, her voice high as she tried to hide her disappointment.

"I've been a guide all over the world," he said. "I've taken travelers through the jungles of South America, the mountains in—"

"How many did you start out with and how many came back?"

Travis's knowing smile made her pulse skip hard. "I haven't lost a client," he said proudly. "There were a few I wanted to push over the cliff, but that's bad for business."

"And what makes you think I need a guide?" she asked, not really sure if she wanted to hear the answer. Did she look lost and out of place? Was it obvious that she didn't know what she was doing?

He had figured her out pretty fast. Did most women visiting Vegas alone feel as if their lives were in a rut? What did they do to get out of it? Something told her that their Vegas to-do list was sexier than hers. That wasn't a surprise. She wasn't a sexy woman and passion never ruled her dating life.

"You're not interested in the gambling or the shows," Travis said. "You want the wild side of Vegas and that isn't so easy to find."

"You don't know what I'm looking for," she pointed out.

Travis's gaze captured hers for a beat. "I have a pretty good idea."

She chuckled. If he knew, he would offer an indecent proposal and the key to his room. It was best that he didn't know. She didn't need any distractions while she tried to cross something off her list.

"I want to do something I haven't done before," she said, rubbing her fingers against her collarbone, belatedly remembering that she'd left her dainty pearl necklace at home. "And I've had so many experiences that I'm sure I've forgotten a few."

"I know the feeling."

He would know. What was she doing pretending to be a worldly woman with this man? Her blood was pumping through her veins harder than it had in a long time. Travis was the real deal. He was going to catch her in a lie.

So what? The question swirled inside her head. *After this weekend, you'll never see him again. Tell outrageous lies and do something daring. If you crash and burn, no one will ever know.*

Yet she still hesitated. "I don't think I can afford you."

Travis's smile grew triumphant. As if he knew he had hooked her and only had to reel her in. "Yes, you can, Christine. I'm giving you this night for free."

That instantly made her suspicious. "Why?"

He shrugged his broad shoulders. "Because I like you."

Sure he did. There had to be a catch somewhere. "Wait, did you say *tonight*? You want to start now?"

"Of course. Did you have other plans?"

She nervously bit her lip. This was the moment when she could find her wilder, more adventurous side. Suddenly the idea of getting settled in her room and having a good night's sleep sounded better. Safer. "Nothing set in stone."

"Then let's go." He pushed away from the slot machine and reached for her.

Christine looked at his hand. It was large and masculine. Rough and weathered. Not the kind that had earned a living working on a computer. "What are we going to do?" She cautiously placed her hand in his.

He closed his fingers around hers and helped her up. "See everything Vegas has to offer."

"That'll take more than one night."

He looked over his shoulder. "That's the plan."

Her instincts told her this guy never had a plan. He was a bad boy looking for trouble. She knew she could see Sin City on her own, but she doubted it would be as much fun as the Vegas Travis knew. She hadn't crossed anything off her list in ten years, but with this man at her side, she'd get more done than she had in a decade.

Christine squared her shoulders and took a deep breath as her stomach twisted with nervousness. "Let's do it."

CHAPTER THREE

SHE WAS SCARED. Travis could tell Christine was trying to act calm but she was almost doubled over with tension. Her breath stuttered as she looked out the window from the top of the Top of the City Hotel and stared down at the Las Vegas Strip. "How high is this jump?"

"Over eight hundred feet," Travis said as he watched Christine close her eyes and whisper something. "More than one hundred floors."

"Yeah, yeah. I got it. It's very high." She pulled uncomfortably at the powder-blue flight suit. "Is it hot in here?"

"No, it's fine," he said. Christine looked very different with her brown hair pulled back in a ponytail and wearing a baggy flight suit. She was adorable, but he had a feeling she wouldn't think that was a compliment.

He heard her groan before she put her hands on her waist and doubled over. He wasn't sure, but Christine looked like she was about to become sick.

Travis felt a sharp pang of guilt. He thought this was a good introduction. A baby step. It wasn't as if she was hurtling out of a plane or BASE jumping. Obviously his idea of a beginner's jump was completely different than hers.

"You're overthinking this," Travis said encouragingly as he rubbed his hand on her back. "It's a very controlled jump. You are hooked up to so many lines and cables. It's like a vertical zip line, but the jump is slowed down so you land safely on the ground."

"Oh, this is so not on my list," she muttered.

"List?" Travis asked. He bent down until his face was level with hers. "What list?"

Christine opened her eyes wide. "What? Nothing." She straightened to her full height.

What kind of list? Travis wondered. It didn't surprise him. Just on the walk along the Strip from the casino, he had learned that Christine Pearson was not a spontaneous person. She was the type who had tunnel vision and to-do lists. "Wait a second, is this a bucket list?"

Christine looked away as her cheeks flushed with embarrassment. "Uh, I guess so. I didn't see it that way. It's just a list of dreams. Things I want to accomplish."

"So basically things you want to do before you kick the bucket. Hence the name," he said as he continued to rub her back. He should stop touching her. He wanted to give her comfort and support but he was very aware of her. His hand glided low on her back and he knew he should stop.

"If you say so," Christine said.

"Why did you make it?" He dropped his hand as he studied her carefully. She was healthy and strong as far as he could tell. "Were you sick?"

"Bored," she replied. She tilted her head and clucked her tongue as if she didn't like that answer. "No, that wasn't it. I wasn't sure what I wanted to do with my life. So I wrote a list of one hundred things that sounded fun."

What did Christine think was fun? He was deeply curious about that. She had been interested in everything she had seen on the Strip. She enjoyed watching people and taking in the sights. She wanted to know more about the street performers who were dressed in silver and acted like statues, and she had never heard about the persistent card clickers who lined the sidewalks offering cards about escort services. Everything was new to her. What was it that she found really exciting? "Like what?" he asked.

She shook her head, refusing to give details. "Some of the stuff on my list are stupid. Not this stupid," she said in a low voice as she looked out the window.

A hundred entries on a bucket list would take time. However, Christine seemed organized, and he had a feeling she didn't dream big. She could have blown through that list in record time. "How many do you have left?"

Christine dipped her head. "A few," she said tightly. "That's one of the reasons I came to Vegas."

"What's on the list?" And why did it require visiting Sin City? Most of the guys he knew would have winning the jackpot in strip poker or skinny-dipping in the Bellagio fountain on their Las Vegas bucket list.

Christine blushed bright pink and looked away. "I'm not telling."

Could her list be just as naughty? No, Christine was too innocent, too much of a lady. She might try to rock a sexier persona but she was a good girl. He didn't know many good girls. What would they want out of life? Probably a husband, kids and a house with a picket fence. The idea sounded claustrophobic to him.

"Become a rock star?" he teased. "Find the end of a rainbow?"

"No," she said with a laugh. "I was eighteen when I put the list together, not six! They're a list of experiences. I wasn't thinking about milestones like graduating high school or getting a driver's license. When my friends were looking at colleges and deciding their career paths, I was planning to backpack across the globe. But I had to put some of those ideas on hold when my dad walked out of our lives. I stayed to look after my mom. You know how it is."

Travis nodded as if he understood, but he didn't think he would have done the same. He had been desperate to break free from his grandmother's strict rules and debilitating fears. When she had died, he had left town after the funeral. He didn't know where he was going to go, but he knew he was not going to end up like his grandmother. He wanted freedom and nothing was going to tie him down.

"By the time Mom got remarried and moved away, I was dating someone who hated traveling." She rubbed her hand over her face, took a deep breath and gave a determined smile. "But now, nothing is holding me back from completing my list."

Travis watched her closely. Christine didn't seem to realize that she had given herself away. She had stayed home. Was she still going to pretend that she was a world traveler?

Why had she stayed home? Travis would never have made that choice. Did Christine love her ex-boyfriend so much that she had given up something she enjoyed? It occurred to him that Aaron was making the same choice to be with Dana. Travis couldn't imagine loving someone so much that he would ignore the wanderlust that drove him.

"So you came to Las Vegas to cross something off your list. And sky jumping isn't on it." He wanted to see that list. It would give him more insight into Christine. "You know, we can go back to the aquarium so you can swim with the sharks."

Christine shook her head vigorously. "Nope, can't do it."

"Really? All you need is a scuba certification. I'm sure you have that."

She snapped her fingers with regret. "I've been so busy. Never should have allowed my scuba certification to expire."

Travis bit back a smile. Anyone who trained to dive underwater would know that scuba certifications never expired. Obviously she was still determined to play this role. He wondered why she felt the need to pretend to be something she wasn't.

"What?" she asked as she watched him with suspicion.

"Nothing," he said. "I'm just glad you don't need any experience to free-fall."

She went pale. "Yeahhh…" The word dragged out of her. "Isn't that great?"

Travis noticed she was beginning to shake. "Christine, are you afraid of heights?"

"No," she said. "I've done some rock climbing."

He held her by the shoulders and bent his head so he could meet her gaze. "You don't have to do this if you don't want to," he said. "You have nothing to prove."

"No, I'm doing this." Travis recognized the determination in her voice. She would regret stepping away from this challenge. "Why aren't you suited up? I thought you liked this kind of thing."

She was right about him. He'd rather climb, jump or run than stand on the sidelines. He needed to push himself to the limit and prove he wouldn't let fear control him. But he wasn't letting anything happen to Aaron's emerald. "I did a free fall once into the water. Without restraints."

Christine's mouth dropped open. *"On purpose?"*

"I didn't plan it. It shredded my clothes." And he wasn't going to tell her about the broken bones and lacerations he got from the fall. "Let's just say it was the better option at that time."

All of her attention was focused on him. She stared into his eyes, hanging on to his words. "I would love to hear all about it," she said quietly.

Christine wanted to know every detail of his travels and mishaps. On the way to the sky jump, she didn't just want to know about the tallest mountain he'd climbed. She wanted to know how he kept going in the face of danger and failure and how it felt to accomplish his goal. No one had asked him that before.

"And I would love to see that bucket list of yours," he replied. What did she hope for? What did she dream about?

Her eyes twinkled at his insistence. "That's not going to happen. There is no comparison."

What did she want to do that could only happen in Las Vegas? What could make her shy about revealing it? Did she want to be a showgirl? Learn illusions from a famous magician? "Then tell me what one thing you've crossed off your list."

"I would but the statute of limitations hasn't expired," she answered primly.

"Christine Pearson?"

Christine flinched, startled, when she heard her name called. She slowly, almost reluctantly, turned to the man who was looking for her. "Yes?"

"You're up next." The guide motioned at the jump platform outside the windows. "Mr. Cain, you can wait with her."

Travis saw Christine's balance wobble as her legs threatened to buckle. He wrapped his arm around her shoulders and held her close. "Christine," he said huskily in her ear, "why do you want to jump?"

WHY DID SHE want to jump? Christine stared at Travis as she considered the question. Was it because she wanted to become an exciting person? Was it because she just wanted to do one stupid thing to tell her friends?

Or was it because she needed to stop making excuses? She made choices knowing it meant she didn't pursue her interests. She had placed other people and goals first. She had delayed her dreams of travel to be there for her mother and, later, for Darrell. She didn't know why she did it, but she had no one to blame but herself.

And because she had stayed in Cedar Valley, she had a job, a home, and belonged to a close community. She was fortunate and she knew it. It took years to get where she was today. She had invested so much time and energy and she didn't want to give that up.

And yet…it felt as if it wasn't her life. It definitely wasn't her dream. She knew she should be grateful, but she wanted more. Something else. She felt she was too young to feel so old. That if she didn't do something now, she would never break free from the routine and predictability.

She slowly raised her head. "I'm jumping because I want to know what it feels like." She wanted to take a risk. Allow the fear and exhilaration to collide inside her. Test her mettle and discover what she could do. When was the last time she did that?

Okay, she had felt a zing of exhilaration when Travis approached her. And when she pretended to be someone else, she hadn't felt that nervous in a long time. But that was different; it had nothing to do with skills or accomplishment. It was simple and instant attraction. Travis Cain was a handsome guy and she was in Vegas. It was a moment when she felt that anything was possible.

"You're going to do great, Christine," Travis called out to her as she walked to the platform. "You'll be fine."

"I don't want to be fine," she said over her shoulder. "I want to shake things up."

Christine stood on the platform and stared out at the Strip. She tasted the fear as she started trembling. She barely heard the man behind her giving tips as he strapped her onto the wires.

"Ready?" the man asked.

She shook her head. Christine stared at the small blue X on the ground, where she was supposed to land. She knew this was a controlled fall, that the wires would keep her on target with where she needed to land, but the ground was so far away.

"You don't have to jump," the man explained. "All you have to do is let go."

He said it as if it was no big deal. That it was perfectly normal to let go of something solid and safe so she could fall to the ground. She took a big breath.

"Don't think about it," the man said. "That will only make it more difficult."

That was her problem in a nutshell. She thought too much. She considered every possibility, every outcome. It didn't take long before she was frozen with indecision and did nothing.

She didn't want to be like that anymore. "I'm ready." Her voice shook.

"Put your toes on the edge. Good. Three…two…one…"

Christine closed her eyes, let go and screamed all the way down.

TRAVIS PACED ON the ground floor as he waited for Christine to change out of her flight suit. He glanced out the window and saw Pitts and Underwood on the sidewalk. They were at a discreet distance as they watched the other sky jumpers.

His instincts told him that they suspected he had the emerald. The stone in his jacket suddenly felt large and heavy. He refused to check his breast pocket. He knew the jewel was deep green and uncut. It was also safely tucked away in a tiny, sealed plastic bag. He didn't know much about gems, but he knew this small emerald was worth a lot of money.

When Aaron first suggested he carry it around in his pocket, Travis thought it was a crazy plan. But it also made sense. Keep the emerald moving with very little fanfare and there was little chance of it getting stolen by Hoffmann. Aaron only needed to show it to an appraiser before the poker game. Once the game was over, Aaron would return home and lock it back up in a safe.

But there was a glitch neither he nor Aaron had considered. Someone had figured out that he had the emerald. Why else would these guys be following him? Travis thought he had lost them when he had taken a bright yellow cab down the traffic-choked street with Christine before they got out and walked the rest of the way. Pitts and Underwood were better than he had expected.

He needed to shake them off before they decided to pounce. He would never forgive himself if Christine got hurt or if he lost the emerald.

"Travis? Is everything okay?"

Travis turned at the sound of Christine's voice. He paused, his chest tightening as he watched her approach. Something had changed about her. She still wore the short blue dress and impractical heels, and her soft brown hair was windblown, but there was no significant alteration in her appearance.

Yet she now walked with a purposeful stride. Her shoulders were back, her head held high as if she was ready to take on the next challenge. A fire had been lit inside her. It was fragile and small. He wanted to see it flare wildly.

"You should be proud of yourself," he said. He knew she had to dig deep and find the courage to take the plunge.

"I am," she admitted with a wide smile. "But my heart is still racing. I don't think my legs have stopped shaking. I thought I was going to throw up after I landed, but that was a false alarm. And my throat hurts."

Travis smiled at how she spoke in quick bursts. He didn't think she was going to be quiet and reserved anymore. The shy Christine had caught his attention, but this side of her was capturing his imagination. "Yeah, you screamed all the way down."

"You would, too." She covered her mouth with her hand. "I can't stop smiling."

He reached for her wrist and pulled her hand away. "Why hide it?"

"Right. Exactly. Why hide it? I just feel strange. Different. Powerful." She gave a husky chuckle. "I'm not making sense, am I?"

"You're making perfect sense," he assured her as he guided her back onto the crowded sidewalk. He knew Christine was still enjoying the excitement of her jump. Her senses were heightened. This was the time when she would be bolder because she felt stronger.

Christine slid her arm through his and held him close. "Everything is so loud. Colorful. I feel like Alice in Wonderland."

Travis looked down at her in surprise. The way she spoke it sounded as if she'd never had an adrenaline rush. How was that possible? People got a high from speeding, having sex and facing their fears. What had she been doing all her life?

He held her arm tighter and led her along the sidewalk. He felt very protective of Christine. She stared at the Las Vegas lights as if everything was becoming brighter. Clearer. Her smile widened. He knew he wanted to see that smile all night long.

"Where to next?" he asked.

She stumbled in her platform heels. "Oh, I shouldn't decide."

"Why not? I'm your guide." He found it curious that she was reluctant to try something more when she seemed so excited about her jump. This was the time when most people would set a bigger challenge for themselves.

"You're supposed to be showing me *your* Las Vegas," she reminded him, her shoulder and hip bumping against him as they strolled down the sidewalk. "Where should we go next?"

He looked around the street, searching for Pitts and Underwood. Dread curled around his abdomen when he couldn't spot them. They could be anywhere. Travis noticed an exotic car idling in the traffic jam and his mind grabbed on to an idea. "Have you ever driven a Ferrari?"

Christine laughed. "I haven't even seen one up close. Why? Do you have one?"

"No, but I know where to borrow one."

She tilted her head and looked at him with narrowed eyes. "When you mean *borrow*..."

"Don't worry, Christine. I won't let you get arrested," he promised. "Not on your first night in Vegas."

CHAPTER FOUR

"THAT WAS INCREDIBLE!" Christine said as they strolled along the sidewalk next to the Bellagio. The night air was cool, but Christine didn't seem to notice as she waved her arms enthusiastically. "I had so much fun."

Travis could tell and he was glad she enjoyed it as much as he did. When he took her to the Las Vegas Motor Raceway to drive exotic cars, he thought she would be careful. Cautious. Slow.

Instead, Christine was a speed demon. His heart had stopped when he watched her take a sharp turn in the Ferrari, but she handled the car beautifully. The woman tested the machine—and his nerves—to the limit. He was sure the tires would have burned from the friction if she'd been allowed to continue.

"Thanks so much for this night, Travis." She wrapped her hands around his arm and leaned into him. "How did you manage to make that happen?" Christine asked.

"I know a guy," he said gruffly as he inhaled her intoxicating scent and his chest clenched. He knew men and women all over the world with whom he bartered and traded favors. They weren't close relationships, but his network of acquaintances and casual friends was an essential part of his nomadic life.

"I wish we could have raced each other," she said.

"That would have been..." *Wild. Electric. Dangerous.* "Interesting." Christine thought she was living on the edge, unaware that he was providing her a protected and safe place.

"I got you something." Christine pulled away and Travis wanted to grasp her hand and draw her back. He watched as she opened her backpack and pulled out a sparkly and colorful keychain. It was the famous diamond-shaped sign that welcomed tourists to Las Vegas. The rhinestones glittered as the chain dangled from her finger.

"Thank you," he said as he accepted it. He held it up and realized that he had no keys to place on the keychain. He didn't own anything that required a key. "I'll think of you every time I look at it."

His statement seemed to please her. "Everyone could use a little more glitter in their lives," she declared.

"I have to know," he said as he slipped the keychain into his pocket. "Where did you learn how to drive like that?"

"I love driving," she said with a sigh as she hooked her arm with his. "Not that you would know it if you saw my car. But whenever I have the chance, I leave town and drive through the mountains. It doesn't take much to encourage me to leave the city limits."

Every time he thought he'd figured out Christine Pearson, she did something that blew apart his theory. She wanted to break free from her comfort zone, but she stayed in her contained world. Something was holding her back. Or was it someone?

There was probably a man back home. Christine was smart, beautiful and joyful. No man would be able to resist her charm. She could have her pick of men and demand everything she wanted. Commitment. Family. A comfortable life.

Everything he avoided. Travis frowned as envy and bitterness churned inside him. He didn't want to think about it. He could give Christine something the men back home could never offer—the thrill of a lifetime and some wild memories. "If I need a driver on my next trip, I'm calling you."

"You're on," Christine said with a wistful smile. She

turned her head and her hand tightened on his arm. "Look! The Bellagio fountain! I see this in the movies all the time!"

Travis indulgently followed Christine as she pulled him to view the fountain up close. He had never stopped to watch the performance. To him, it was simply water moving to music, but he could understand why Christine would be fascinated. He enjoyed seeing the world through her eyes.

Everything was beautiful to Christine. She found pleasure in the stores that sold kitschy souvenirs and in the fries she ate at a retro diner. And yet, she wasn't ready to live hard and fast, making up for lost time. She wanted to savor every moment.

They stood with the crowd and watched the water-and-lights display. After a few moments, Travis found himself watching Christine. Her expressions fascinated him.

Her brown eyes widened as the water sprayed to unbelievable heights. Her face softened at the cheesy romantic song. Her satisfied sigh pierced his heart. Travis wanted to hear that sound again. He wanted to make her sigh like that just for him.

The breeze pulled at her dark hair. Without thinking, Travis reached out and grasped the long tresses that buffeted her face. Her hair was as soft as he had expected.

His heart started to pound as he tucked her hair back. He dragged his finger along the curve of her ear and felt her shiver of delight. Christine slowly turned toward him as the song continued to play. Her eyes darkened as she shyly met his gaze.

Travis didn't say anything as he slid his fingers along her jaw and cradled her face with his hands. Her lips parted as his mouth grazed hers.

He had meant for it to be a brush of lips, a whisper of a kiss. He didn't expect the crackle of fire between them. It promised something wild and uncontrollable.

Christine tasted of innocence and mystery. Heat and softness. It was like nothing he'd ever experienced before. His skin tingled and he felt that kick of excitement as she yielded and drew him past her lips.

He deepened the kiss as the lust licked through his veins. He dimly heard the flourishing end of the song and the crash of water. All he noticed was how Christine melted into him. The crowd dispersed, jostling them. He instinctively held her close to protect her as someone bumped into him. She clutched his jacket lapel as she hungrily returned his kiss. Travis wasn't ready to end this. He gathered her against him until her soft curves were flush with his rock-hard body.

Travis knew they were too far from the hotel. He wanted somewhere quiet and private where he could explore Christine inch by inch. Shed their clothes and…

Tension gripped his muscles as he realized he missed something. Something important. He suddenly recalled that someone had bumped right up against him.

The crowd hadn't been that packed. Dread settled deep in his gut. Was it one of the guys who had followed them earlier? Did they know he had the emerald in his breast pocket?

Travis abruptly pulled away from Christine. He had to stop himself from checking the emerald. Alarm scorched through him and it must have shown as he saw Christine's guarded expression.

"I'm sorry," he said hoarsely as he watched Christine press her fingertips against her swollen lips. "I shouldn't have done that."

"There's nothing to be sorry about," she said as desire shimmered in her eyes. "You did that very well."

He tilted his head as hope leaped into his chest. He wanted to pursue what was happening between them right now. Travis was about to reach for Christine when his cell phone buzzed. He gritted his teeth and swallowed back a growl of frustration. "I have to get this."

Christine lowered her gaze. "Not a problem."

He surreptitiously checked for the emerald as he retrieved

his cell phone from his pocket, and wanted to sag with relief when he felt the stone. He glanced at the phone and saw Aaron's number. He wasn't surprised. It was a shock that his friend hadn't contacted him until now.

Travis answered his phone. "Hello?" he asked curtly. He didn't want any more interruptions.

"Travis? How's it going?" Aaron asked.

"Good. Why?" Travis heard the underlying tension in his friend's voice. He glanced around the sidewalk. Pitts and Underwood were nowhere to be seen.

"Okay." Aaron's voice dropped to a confiding whisper. "You know how I said you were paranoid because you thought those two guys were watching us."

"Yeah?" He did another quick survey of the area. Nothing.

"Well, I think someone was in my hotel room."

Travis's head came up like an animal scenting danger. It must have been obvious as Christine looked at him with concern. He flashed her a lopsided smile as if nothing was wrong. "How do you know?"

"I did the toothpick trick you showed me," Aaron said in a rush. "You know, put the toothpick on the top of the door and close it."

"Found it on the floor, huh?" He didn't need confirmation. He knew the room had been searched.

"Yes! I also did it for the bathroom door and the closet. They're all on the floor. I got out of there as fast as I could and called you."

"Do you need me to drop by?" Travis asked. He saw Christine's chin dip with disappointment.

"Actually…" Aaron's tone changed. "I need my emerald now before the game starts."

Travis rubbed his forehead as he tried to understand his friend's insistence on playing the game with the questionable group. Did he think this emerald had some protective spell? "You're still going through with it?"

"Yes, of course," Aaron replied. "And then I'll give the stone right back to you. What could go wrong?"

Travis groaned. "Famous last words."

"You sound different," Aaron said.

He probably did. He hadn't felt this frustrated in a long time. He was used to getting what he wanted, when he wanted it. But now he couldn't follow up on this attraction that flared between him and Christine. "No," he said through clenched teeth. "I'm good."

"Wait a second," Aaron said slyly. "Are you still with that hot chick?"

He glanced at Christine and their gazes held. "Yes."

"Seriously?" his friend said in a high-pitched squawk. "How the hell did you get her to go with you?"

He couldn't answer that because he had no idea. "I'll be right there," he promised with great reluctance before he disconnected the call.

"You have to leave?" Christine asked.

"I have to drop by the casino," he said as he placed the cell phone into his pocket. "It won't take long."

"No, that's fine." She took a step back and crossed her arms. "I've already taken up enough of your time."

"I'm not ready to call it a night," he said. Especially after that kiss. "I have to do something for a friend and then I'll take you dancing."

Her eyes widened. "Dancing? Like at a nightclub?"

He nodded. She looked as nervous as she had when she suited up for the sky jump. He couldn't imagine why. "I know, I know, you've seen one nightclub, you've seen them all. But I promise, this one is different."

"Dancing?" she repeated. She snapped her mouth shut and flipped back her hair. "Eh, sounds a little tame, Travis."

He gave her a slow, wicked smile. "Then you're not doing it right."

NOT DOING IT RIGHT. Christine nervously thought about Travis's words as they stepped into the nightclub an hour later. It was more like not doing it at all.

She looked around the nightclub. It wasn't like anything she had expected, but then she had never been to a club. They didn't have any around Cedar Valley.

The place was obviously popular, but she wasn't sure why. The white walls, pink lights and sheer curtains didn't look exotic or mysterious. The live band was good but she didn't recognize any of the music. The dance floor was filled with men and women her age, their hands up in the air as they swayed to the beat. Christine's shoulders tightened as she surveyed the unfamiliar setting. She didn't know the latest dance moves or what drink to order.

She glanced at Travis, who stood by her side. He had changed into a dark suit and a gray shirt. Christine bit her bottom lip as she looked at her blue dress. It was limp and tired. She hadn't considered changing. Should she have? This was really the only dress she had to go clubbing.

She frowned. Was she even using the correct verb? Did they use the term *clubbing* anymore? She just didn't know.

Christine knew she shouldn't be this nervous, but it had been so long since she had danced. Dancing meant losing control and surrendering to the music. It revealed what was going on inside her. She couldn't show that, not back at home.

She always had to be on her best behavior in Cedar Valley. She had discovered that when she first started working at the bank. Her community wanted to know that she was a reliable and serious person. That they could trust her. People had no sense of humor when it came to their money and valuables. And for good reason. But now it had gone too far and for too long. She'd lost a piece of her identity in the process. A sense of her true self.

Christine had yielded to the town's expectations because she needed the job. She thought it was going to be temporary, but she had stayed and didn't recognize the gradual shift in herself during the years. The flirty clothes she used to wear were replaced with appropriate work attire in dull colors. She never did anything "out there" or that caused a scene, no matter how much she wanted to. But did any of it pay off? No. Instead of being rewarded for her efforts, her life was in a rut.

That needed to change, even if it meant continuing to take wild weekends away from Cedar Valley. It was going to be a balancing act to keep everything she'd worked hard for and still fulfill her dreams. As fascinating as Travis's life sounded, she knew it wasn't for her. She needed a safety net and a place to call home.

"What do you think?" Travis asked, his mouth close to her ear.

Christine shivered with anticipation as his warm breath caressed her skin. She couldn't wait for him to kiss her again. She didn't know if that was going to happen, but she couldn't make the next move. Old habits died hard.

"It's great." Christine looked around and saw quite a few bachelorette parties on the floor. She looked at the bar and noticed two men staring at her. It wasn't a flirtatious look or even one of interest. They were watchful as they zeroed in on her among all the other women in the club.

They looked familiar but she wasn't sure why. "Do you know those guys?" she asked Travis, gesturing with a nod of her head. "They keep looking at us."

Travis gave a quick glance. "No, never met them," he said tightly. "Come on, let's dance."

Travis grasped her elbow and led her onto the dance floor. There was barely any room, yet he managed to cut through the crowd with ease. She envied that skill. She imagined he didn't have any trouble finding a path through a maze or a jungle.

A stunning woman with silky red hair gave him a long, lingering glance. Travis didn't seem to notice. The redhead was sleek and sophisticated in a little black dress. She was a symbol of effortless elegance, and Christine couldn't compete. She felt like a broken-down car next to a Ferrari.

Christine hesitated, but Travis gently pulled her forward. Why was Travis with her? He could have any woman he wanted. Was it because he thought she was a kindred spirit? Bold, adventurous and wild? She hoped he never found out the truth.

Travis stopped in the middle of the dance floor and turned around. Christine's heart began to pump hard as he gathered her close in his arms. Her body was on full alert as she curled her arms over his shoulders. She was surrounded by him. His scent, his heat. Christine looked away, unable to meet his gaze. She felt safe and protected in the sea of people and yet she felt just as she had when she'd been on the edge of the Top of the City Hotel, ready to let go and fall.

She wanted to pursue this. Pursue Travis. It didn't make sense. She didn't have flings. She had relationships. Loving, committed relationships with a future. She wasn't thinking about that with Travis.

And yet, she wanted him more than she wanted to check something off her list. But she couldn't repeat that mistake. She couldn't allow a man to distract her from a goal. When she had delayed her dreams for Darrell, she had considered the pros and cons. She thought it had been the right decision to stay in Cedar Valley and make their relationship a priority.

A lot of good that did. She should have put herself and her dreams first. This time her dream list was top priority. She wanted Travis more than she wanted to climb Mount Rainier or get a tattoo, but she simply couldn't leave Vegas with nothing crossed off her dream list.

As she followed Travis's movements, her breasts brushing against his chest, Christine fought back the urge to roll her hips against his. She hadn't crossed anything off her list and she had only two more days here.

What if she crossed one thing off her list before exploring

this thing with Travis? The excitement started to fizz through her veins as she grabbed hold of this idea. Just one. That was all she needed. Complete one goal and then she could add Travis to her list.

"You look very serious all of a sudden," Travis said against her ear.

A one-night stand. But it wasn't enough. She wanted more than one night, one time.

"Relax," he continued. "I won't let anything happen to you."

But she wanted something to happen. Something that would change her life. Her point of view.

"I was thinking I haven't checked anything off my list since I got to Vegas," she said. What would be the easiest thing to accomplish? Something quick. She didn't want to waste any more time. The sooner she crossed something off her list, the sooner she could start her wild night with Travis.

"We'll have to do something about that," he said as his hands slid down the small of her back. "What's on your list?"

You. And by this time tomorrow, Travis Cain will have been added and checked off her list. "How do you feel about the Grand Canyon?"

"I can make that happen." Travis said.

Christine smiled. "I know you can."

CHAPTER FIVE

WHAT WAS HE doing wrong? Travis had Christine in the palm of his hand last night. She had been so attuned to his body that they moved as one on the dance floor without thinking about it.

It was obvious that she didn't want the night to end, yet she went to her hotel room alone. Today she'd refrained from touching him, as if she'd been having second thoughts. He had felt her hot gaze on him, had caught the yearning looks before she glanced away, but she'd kept her distance all morning and afternoon.

It had been agony to be on his best behavior all day, Travis thought as he watched Christine feed another dollar into the slot machine. He knew he had to keep moving to avoid Pitts and Underwood, but all he really wanted to do was stop time, find a private corner and pull Christine back into his arms.

"It's official. Lady Luck hates me," Christine announced as she raised her hands and glared at the slot machine. "That's all there is to it. The world knows what I want and won't let me have it."

"An extreme view," Travis said with a smile. And he knew it was a temporary one. He wondered when she would show a sign of exasperation. They'd had a streak of bad luck, but Christine didn't allow it to slow her down. She kept looking for the next adventure.

This time she was dressed as if prepared for anything. Her hair was pulled back in a ponytail and she wore sneakers. Her tight jeans accentuated her long legs, and her snug hot-pink T-shirt had the words *Las Vegas* emblazoned on the front. As much as he enjoyed the sight of her in the blue dress and high heels, he had a feeling this casual look was more like her.

Travis glanced at his watch and knew they were running out of time. Night was about to fall and Christine had to check out of the hotel tomorrow at noon to catch her flight home. They had spent most of the day trying to find one thing Christine could cross off her list.

Little did she know that he was slowly piecing together her dream list and getting an intimate view of her. She had a fascination with speed and a fear of fire. She felt more comfortable with nature than in an urban setting. And for a woman who seemed to have a lot of friends, Christine didn't include them in her dreams. All her goals could be done solo.

"I'm sorry." She pressed her lips together and shook her head. "I didn't mean that. I've been having a great time. I really have. I loved driving the Ferrari, and I can't believe I jumped off a building. I can't wait to tell Jill about that."

Jill. Her best friend, who owned a dry-cleaning store. It felt as if he knew every citizen in Cedar Valley now. It sounded like the kind of quaint town he'd seen only in the movies. The kind where no one locked their doors and everyone looked out for one another. The kind of place that would make him feel claustrophobic. "She won't believe you," he said.

"Probably not. That's okay, because I know I did it," Christine said. Her proud smile faded. "But I wanted to check *one* thing off my list. I won't forgive myself if I don't do it. I set aside this weekend to work on it. If I fail in that endeavor, what does it say about me?"

"Nothing. It says something about the goals," he said as he curled his arm around her shoulders and guided her away from the slot machine. He wanted to draw her closer but knew he'd be pushing his luck. "It can take time to achieve one. It could also mean that you have to modify a goal."

"You mean downsize it?" Christine shook her head. "No, that's cheating. That's not what my list is about. It's about going for it. No compromising. No holding back."

"The list you won't let me see." He said it in a teasing tone, but her secrecy was starting to bother him. Why didn't she trust him with her dreams? She still seemed uncomfortable with his help. Did she suspect he had an ulterior motive? Or was she not used to having support?

"You know some of it," she muttered as her cheeks turned red. "I wrote it knowing no one else would see it. Some of those goals are private."

"I understand. When I was growing up, I wanted to climb Mount Everest. I told my friends and they thought it was a joke. They didn't think I could do it. They didn't think I would leave home." A goal revealed a lot about a person. It was more than pushing the limit or boundaries. It showed not only their heart's desire, but also what they lacked in life. What they wanted more than anything. Travis had learned to be careful in telling someone his dream and revealing why he kept challenging himself. It had been his way of protecting himself. He didn't want anyone to say his goals were never going to happen.

"And you left home. You showed them. What are your goals now?"

"Never return home. Never stop moving." Travis sighed and shook his head to rid himself of those thoughts. "Okay, the helicopter ride to the Grand Canyon fell through." That had been bad luck that all the helicopters were grounded due to high winds. "So did the land sailing. We could zip-line down Boulder Canyon."

Christine shook her head. "It sounds like fun, but it's not on my list."

"Here's a thought," he said, leaning toward her and whispering theatrically. "Ignore the list."

"Right now I would love to." She glanced up at him, and

he saw the glitter of desire in her eyes. She determinedly turned her head away. "But tomorrow I'll wake up and wish I had stayed focused."

"There's nothing wrong with adapting. I had to learn that skill when I first started traveling. Some of my best times happen when I ignore my itinerary."

Christine stopped and gave him a look, raising her eyebrow. "You don't strike me as a guy who would have an itinerary."

She would be surprised. He had a clear itinerary for what he would like to do with her. First he would drag that rubber band from her ponytail and sink his hands into her soft brown hair. Then he would tilt her head back and claim her mouth with his…. The air hissed between his teeth as he grew hard. He was willing to adapt and make changes as long as it ended up with them naked, in bed and satisfied.

"I think of them as ideas. Suggestions. They aren't set in stone," Travis said. His chest tightened as he decided to follow an impulse. "You know, you could extend your vacation."

He saw the pleasure bloom in Christine's face at his words. Just when he thought she was considering the option, the light dimmed in her eyes and the corner of her mouth tightened. "No, that's not going to happen," she said as the sadness tinged her voice. "I have to leave tomorrow."

"Come on," Travis wheedled. He was also going to leave tomorrow and get ready for his next adventure, but he would delay his trip if it meant being with Christine. "What's the worst thing that could happen if you missed your plane?"

Christine shuddered. "I don't want to even think about it."

He wasn't surprised by her response, but he wanted her to consider it. He wanted more time with Christine. "Maybe the question should be, how important is it for you to cross something off your list?"

"It's important," she said with great urgency. "I can't begin to tell you how important it is. Ooh. Another slot machine."

She ran over and fed the machine a dollar. Travis stood by her side, arms crossed as he shook his head. As the bells rang and the symbols rolled, he caught the reflection of Pitts and Underwood several machines away.

Damn. Travis gritted his teeth. He was still being followed. He hadn't seen them all day. Either they were getting better at surveillance or he was getting too distracted with Christine.

Fear twisted in his stomach. He knew Pitts and Underwood weren't going to follow for much longer. They were going to make their move very soon. The high-stakes poker game was going to be over tonight. He needed to find a way to stay in a public and crowded area.

After this weekend, he was not going to babysit the emerald for Aaron again. Even if the next poker game was in Macau or if Aaron offered more money. His friend knew Hoffmann was after the emerald. The guy had to get over his suspicions about hotel security or hire a true professional.

Christine's shoulders slumped as she lost again. "I don't understand," she said. "I should have won something by now. Even a quarter. A penny. I don't care as long as it's something."

"You've been feeding these machines all day," Travis said. "I think it's time to take a break."

"It's on my list," Christine admitted. "Win money is number forty-three."

He stared at her. That was the kind of goal she had? It didn't make sense to him. "What kind of wild adventure is winning money?"

"It's not." She shrugged. "This is why I don't share my list. Some of the goals aren't exciting. But they are my dreams and there's usually a reason behind them. I added 'win money' because it was always a struggle to get the cash to go on a trip."

"Well, that would explain why you have difficulty walking past a slot machine. It's good to know I don't have to stage an intervention." Travis shoved his hands through his hair as he thought about her goal. The odds weren't good for this dream, but he understood it. After all, he was babysitting an emerald to pay for a trip to Indonesia. "If you want to win money, try something different."

"No, I give up." She turned and strode away from the row of slot machines. "Win money was my backup goal in Vegas. I've wasted too much time on something that isn't going to happen."

Travis hurried to catch up with her. "Now isn't the time to give up. It's the time to adapt. Change course," he encouraged her. "Try blackjack or roulette. Throw some dice."

"Those games are too expensive," she said.

"Too expensive to fulfill one goal?" Travis never allowed anything to get in the way of accomplishing a dream. There were times when he took a gamble and failed, but he wasn't afraid of losing it all. He knew he could recover and start over.

"Yes," she said definitively. "I don't want to go all in."

"You should try it once," he insisted. "The adrenaline rush makes it all worth it."

"I've gone all in before," she said as her expression darkened. "Gave it everything I had. Sacrificed more than I should and it still hurts. I haven't recovered."

Travis had a feeling she wasn't talking about gambling.

"No more slot machines," Christine stated with determined cheerfulness. "Let's go to the Mirage and see the white tiger exhibit. I know it's not as exciting as zip-lining, but we might come up with an idea while we're there."

"I'm already having fun." And it was true. He enjoyed being with Christine. He didn't miss the rush of an extreme sport or fight the need to keep moving. Instead, he wanted to linger, stay in one place and gain Christine's full attention.

"I know you said I don't have to pay you, but I still—" Christine bumped into a tall, thin man. "Oh, excuse me."

"I'm sorry. Are you all right?" The man had a faint accent that Travis couldn't place. He frowned as he noticed the man's baseball cap and sunglasses.

Travis immediately recognized him. It was Underwood, dressed casually and keeping his head down as he boldly made contact. Underwood expertly slid his hand across Christine while pretending to hold her steady. Underwood's hand splayed against her wrist bag in a classic pickpocket move.

Travis grabbed her hand, blocking Underwood from completing the theft. Travis's stealth move revealed his training, but he had no choice in the matter. His protective instincts had kicked in and he wasn't going to allow this man anywhere near Christine.

He knew Pitts would be nearby. One glance in Underwood's sunglasses and Travis saw the guy right behind them. He and Christine had to get out of there before Pitts and Underwood discovered the emerald in his shirt pocket.

"Let's go," Travis told Christine as he quickly pulled her away. He needed to find a spot that had heavy security.

"Sorry!" she called out to Underwood over her shoulder. "Wow, I swear that guy came out of nowhere."

That was close. He should have predicted it, but he was taken by surprise that they had gone after Christine. Why did they think she had the emerald? Unless it was a move to distract him so Pitts could pick his pockets.

Travis's hands shook as he escorted Christine to the entrance. He realized it wasn't adrenaline flowing through his veins. It was fear. He had placed Christine in danger. What if Pitts or Underwood had a weapon? How would he have protected her?

This babysitting job was over. He was returning the emerald to Aaron immediately. "I have to make a call before we go," he said to Christine.

"Sure," she said as she headed directly to the slot machine by the entrance. "I'm going to give this one more try."

"So much for quitting," he said with a smile. He turned

around and scoped out the casino. Dressed like the other weekend tourists, Pitts or Underwood couldn't be spotted in the crowd. Travis reached for the phone in his jacket pocket and casually checked for the emerald in his shirt pocket. It was still there. He didn't care if Aaron thought it brought good luck. He couldn't wait to get rid of it.

As he dialed, Travis heard loud bells and whistles. Someone had hit the jackpot nearby. Someone whooped with sheer joy. It sounded a lot like Christine. Travis slowly turned and saw her jumping up and down.

"I won!" she shouted as he stared wordlessly at the flashing lights on the slot machine. "I finally won!"

"I WON!" CHRISTINE couldn't stop smiling as she crammed the cash into her small purse. "I won. I won. I won."

"I'm as stunned as you are," Travis said as he pressed his hand against her back and guided her out of the casino.

"I can't believe I won." She was excited. Relieved. She'd completed a challenge and was ready to accept the reward. "I have no idea what to do with this money."

"This is Vegas," he reminded her. They stood on the sidewalk and inhaled the desert air. "Where do you want to go? You can get almost anything. Clothes. Jewelry. Or do you want to gamble some more?"

"No, none of that interests me." It was only a few hundred dollars, but she knew she wasn't going to put it away for a rainy day. She wanted to use it on something fun with Travis. "It doesn't matter. I won!"

More important, she could cross entry number forty-three—win money—off her list. A satisfied sigh staggered from her throat. She was almost light-headed with relief. Tomorrow she could return home knowing she had accomplished what she had set out to do.

The sun was beginning to set and the golden lights reflected on the buildings. Her weekend was almost up, but she wasn't ready to go home. Not when she could add Travis to her dream list.

She imagined the entry on her list. One hundred and one: Travis. Not a one-night stand. Not a fling. Simply Travis. She didn't care how she got him as long as he wound up in her bed.

But she didn't have that much time. How was she going to do it? The idea made her jittery and nervous. He thought she was a sophisticated and mysterious woman. She wasn't that experienced. Her last boyfriend had dumped her because she wasn't exciting enough for him.

"It's your choice, Christine," Travis said. "What do you want to do?"

She took a deep breath. She wasn't going to talk herself out of this. She always did that and then regretted it.

But this time she needed to make the first move. That was completely out of her comfort zone. She never grabbed what she wanted. She always waited for permission. For her turn.

Forget that. This was her chance. It was time for her to take a risk. If she didn't do this, she would regret missing the opportunity.

"Travis?" she said, her voice sounding high to her ears. He must have heard it, too. Travis went still and cast a quick glance at her.

She wasn't sure what to say. Maybe this was one of those times when words weren't necessary. Her chest rose and fell with each uneven breath as she took a step forward. Travis watched her intently, but he remained silent.

Christine slid her hands over his chest. He was warm and muscular. She frowned when her hand bumped against something solid in his shirt pocket. His fingers suddenly wrapped around her wrists. For a moment she couldn't tell if he was going to reject her advances.

This wasn't going as well as she had hoped. She had expected him to meet her halfway. Sweep her up into his arms and kiss her. But did a worldly, mysterious woman allow the man to take charge? She doubted it. If she wanted Travis, she would have to act like her alter ego.

Christine's heart was pounding ferociously as she leaned forward and kissed him. She meant for it to be bold and powerful, but the moment her lips touched his, she softened against him. Her mouth clung to him as she felt his surprise.

Travis dropped her wrists and held her face in his calloused hands. She tasted the urgency, the pulsating need as he gave her a hard, possessive kiss. She wanted to melt into him when he lifted his head.

"What were you saying, Christine?" he asked hoarsely as his eyes glittered with desire. She felt the throbbing response deep in her belly. No man had looked at her like that before.

She curled her hands against his shoulders. He felt strong and solid underneath her touch. "I don't feel like sightseeing anymore."

His mouth tilted up into a wicked smile. "What do you want to do?"

She suddenly felt shy. Christine looked away and paused. She was a brazen and sophisticated woman, she reminded herself. Christine slowly lifted her head and met Travis's gaze. "I want to take you back to my room."

"Lead the way."

CHAPTER SIX

CHRISTINE DIDN'T SPEAK to Travis as she led him to her room. Words were jumbled in her mind and her throat felt tight and thick. She felt awkward and clumsy as she slid the key card into the lock. She experienced a wave of relief as the green light flickered, and her hands trembled as she wrenched the door open.

She stepped inside her dark hotel room and turned around. Travis stood in the doorway, his hands bracing the frame. His eyes were piercing. She felt the urgency ripple from his body, but he waited for her to make the next move.

"Invite me in," he said roughly.

He knew. He knew that she was nervous. She was afraid to reach for the opportunity only to have it disappear—or, worse, confirm her fears that she wasn't exciting. That she wasn't good in bed.

But she hadn't felt like this with another man. And Travis was hers for the taking. He had been since the moment they met next to the slot machine. She'd only needed the courage to take the next step. Reach out and claim him.

"I'll wait." His voice was a rasp. "It's not going to be easy. I want you now, but I will wait until you make the first move."

Christine shivered. She didn't realize how important it was for her to hear those words. She needed to know that he wanted this as much as she did. But she wanted it to be memorable for Travis. This one-night stand was going to mean more to her than to him.

"Travis…"

"I know this could be from the adrenaline rush of winning." He reached out and cupped her cheek with his warm and large hand.

She didn't want to move away. "It's not. I've wanted this since I first met you."

"What is stopping you?" he asked as he brushed his thumb against her cheekbone. His touch was as light as a feather. "Is there someone back home?"

She wanted to live out this fantasy but she wasn't very brave. Not in Cedar Valley and not in bed. It was easier to act as if her fantasies didn't exist than to go after them. She wished it wasn't so difficult to surrender to the moment.

"There's no one else," she said.

Travis bent his head and gave her the gentlest of kisses. His mouth grazed hers and color exploded inside her. She parted her lips as her breath hitched in her throat.

If his kiss had been hard and demanding, she would have pulled away. She would have told him she had changed her mind and asked him to leave. It would have been her biggest regret, but this kiss proved that Travis could be a tender and patient lover.

She slowly pulled away. Her heart pounded in her ears. She felt as though she was letting go of something safe and solid. Taking a risk that could have her soaring or falling. "Come inside," she whispered.

Her pulse skipped a beat as she reached for his hand. Christine entwined their fingers, hers looking small and pale next to his. The sight made her heart twist. She wanted to hold on to him. Become one with him.

Christine looked into Travis's eyes. She saw the desire and the hope. She led him across the threshold and welcomed him by curling her arms around his strong shoulders. He kissed with great care as he gathered her close. Her kisses grew bolder. Christine pushed his jacket off his broad shoulders and unbuttoned his shirt as he kicked off his shoes. She stripped him quickly before she lost her nerve. She felt the strength of his muscular chest and his hard arousal. She rocked her hips with anticipation, and Travis groaned against her mouth.

She didn't speak as he slowly peeled her clothes from her body. It was as if he was unwrapping a gift. By the time she was naked, she was trembling and craving his touch. She was desperate for his mouth. For him.

Travis led her to the bed and lowered her gently as if she was a delicate treasure. Her spine sank into the soft mattress and she drew him down with her. Travis lay at her side, watching her intently as she explored his body with her hands and mouth. She learned what made him sigh with pleasure and what made him clench with barely leashed restraint. Most of all, she discovered Travis's patience matched her insatiable curiosity.

When Travis couldn't take it anymore, he covered her body with his. Christine wrapped her hands around his penis and couldn't suppress the ripple of excitement. She loved the feel of him, enjoyed the pulsating heat and strength under her fingertips.

"Tell me what you want," Christine said as she arched against him. She pressed her mouth against his throat and felt his fast pulse under her lips.

"Show me how you feel," Travis said huskily. "Don't hold back."

Christine reached for his hands, which were flattened on the bed next to her head. She laced her fingers with his and held on tight. She tilted her head and sought his mouth. Christine gave him the sweetest kiss.

She didn't want to hold back but she was scared. The sensations swirling inside her felt stronger than her. The coiling desire held such promise but she fought it. She knew if she allowed it to take over, she would never be the same.

Travis ended the kiss and looked into her eyes. His eyes

glittered with an intensity that made her pause. He seemed mesmerized by the emotions chasing across her face.

Christine didn't want to be the same person she had been before this trip. She wanted to feel, to know. She knew he would guide her to the height of pleasure and hold her when she fell. Travis would take care of her and not let go.

TRAVIS WAS INSTANTLY aware of the moment she yielded. She whispered and sighed as he caressed her. She encouraged him with incomplete sentences when he explored her with his mouth. Soon she guided him with her hands. He knew what she wanted with the roll of her hips and the arch of her spine.

His body strained for completion as he stared into Christine's eyes. He couldn't get enough of her untamed reactions. He wanted to capture this rare moment.

Travis quickly slipped on protection and settled between her legs as the lust kicked hard. Victory and gratitude rushed through his veins, but when he held Christine's gaze, he was humbled by her trust. He was going to do everything he could to be worthy of it. Worthy of her.

Travis grasped her hips and sank into her welcoming body. He tilted his head back as the primitive instincts stormed through him. Christine's eyes glimmered with stark need as she bucked beneath him.

The fascination he felt for this woman almost scared him. He thrust into her and shuddered at the sound of her earthy groan. He knew once she submitted to him that she would reach a new level of pleasure. He thrust again and watched in awe as Christine climaxed in his arms.

She hid nothing. He saw the reckless spirit in her eyes as she went wild beneath him. She was fire—primal, uninhibited beauty.

He couldn't hold on for much longer, but he wanted more. He needed more time to explore this connection and this woman. As the scorching pleasure ripped through him, Travis knew he had to convince Christine to stay.

THE NEXT MORNING, Christine stared at the alarm clock on the bedside table and swallowed back a groan. *I'm late. This is a disaster. I can't be late.*

The words rushed through her mind as she hurriedly buttoned up her white long-sleeved shirt and shoved the long hem in her navy blue pants. How could this have happened? She was never late. She always woke up at dawn and had everything prepared ahead of time to ensure an easygoing morning.

But last night wasn't routine. If she took a man like Travis to her bed every night, she wouldn't seek adventure elsewhere. Her skin tingled and her stomach clenched as she remembered how he had touched her. She had never slept with a man as sexual, as tender or as knowledgeable as Travis Cain.

She hadn't been able to keep her hands off him. He didn't seem to mind that she woke him up several times throughout the night to make love. It was almost as if she needed to be certain it hadn't been a dream.

And this morning, she had woken up as the sun streaked through the gap in the curtains. This time she didn't awaken Travis. Instead she'd lain next to him, cherishing the moment, holding on to the fantasy until she had to get up and get back to reality.

Christine reached up and gathered her hair in a tight topknot as she studied Travis in her bed. The bedsheets were startlingly white against his golden-brown skin. He was sprawled across the mattress, his arms outstretched and his feet dangling off the corner.

The blanket was a tangled mess and barely covered his hips. She couldn't stop staring at his powerful thighs and tapered waist. Her fingers itched, eager to caress his well-defined abdominal muscles.

He was gloriously male and naked. She missed seeing his

body last night. They hadn't taken the time to turn on the lights. Christine had felt the crisp curls on his broad chest and heard the strong beat of his heart when she curled up against him. She hadn't seen the dark stubble on his jaw, but her lips were still red from the friction.

Christine paused. She rubbed her hand against her collarbone and her fingers brushed against her neckline. She was tempted to shed her clothes and crawl back in bed. Why shouldn't she miss her flight? No one was waiting for her at home. The bank could survive a day without her.

What was she thinking? She had allowed a man to distract her from her plan before. She wasn't going to let it happen again. Christine pulled at her collar and realized she had released the top button. She quickly fixed her top and marched to the bathroom. She scooped her toiletries into her arm and hurried back to her suitcase.

After all, this was a one-night stand. Nothing more. She'd never had one before and didn't know the rules, but Travis wasn't looking for a relationship. He knew she was returning home today.

And if she extended her vacation, she would only find disappointment. At the moment Travis found her interesting. Anyone could pretend to be for a couple of days, but she couldn't maintain her sophisticated persona for much longer. She had already slipped up multiple times and it was only by incredible luck that he hadn't noticed. It wouldn't take him long to realize what kind of person she truly was—an average woman who dreamed big but lived small.

Christine slipped her feet into her loafers and looked around the hotel room. It was small, plain and beige, but she didn't think she would remember that. She would remember the kaleidoscope of colors and emotions she'd experienced here. She'd cherish the memory of how alive and daring she felt in Travis's arms.

She dipped her head and took a deep breath. She had to

get out of here now if she wanted to make her flight. Christine glanced at the door and saw the pile of clothes on the carpeted floor. How could she have missed that?

Rushing over to the door, she grabbed her clothes from the top of the pile and tossed them into her suitcase. She zipped up her luggage and cringed when the metallic sound echoed in the quiet room. Glancing over at the bed, Christine went very still until she saw that Travis was still sleeping soundly.

She was overwhelmed with the urge to wake him up and say goodbye. She wanted to thank him for showing her Vegas, for encouraging her to pursue her dreams and for taking the time to make sure she crossed something off her bucket list. But, most of all, she wanted one more kiss.

Christine pressed her lips together. No, she shouldn't do that. It would start a chain reaction. She squared her shoulders and thrust out her chin. All he would have to do was look at her and she would stay.

And then she might find out the truth that would crack through her dream weekend. She felt something more than desire, but that didn't mean Travis felt the same way. She could keep the fantasy but that meant getting out of here before she ruined this beautiful memory.

Christine's eyelashes fluttered as she felt the sting of tears. She wasn't going to regret leaving. She would regret it more if she tried to extend this one-night stand. She grabbed her suitcase and quietly left, refusing to look back.

TRAVIS WOKE UP when he heard the buzz of his cell phone. He gradually opened his eyes and stared at the white ceiling. It took a moment for him to notice the stream of sunlight. His need to turn over and go back to sleep evaporated when he realized he didn't recognize the room.

He sat up and looked around. The hotel room was like any other. He looked at the bed and saw the dent on the pillow next to him. He smiled as the memories came rushing back. "Christine?"

She didn't answer. The bathroom and closet doors were ajar, as if they'd been thrown open in a hurry. Travis reluctantly looked at the clock on the table next to the bed. It was past noon.

Damn. Travis tiredly rubbed his hand over his jaw, the stubble scratching his palm. She must have left for the airport. The disappointment weighed heavily in his chest. He hadn't had a chance to say goodbye.

In a hazy way, he recalled encouraging her to stay for another day, but she hadn't seemed interested. He should have gotten her phone number or email address. Anything that gave him the chance to continue what they had shared. Now that link had been broken. She was gone.

The regret was unfamiliar. He was used to keeping relationships casual. They were meant to be fun, sexy and temporary. But it felt different with Christine. What they shared was more of a connection. Something he hadn't felt with anyone for a long time. And when she curled up against him, showing her trust... Travis exhaled sharply. Well, he thought it was more than a hookup.

He heard the buzz of his cell phone again and tilted his head. It sounded like it was close to the door. He rose to his feet and stretched. Looking around, Travis hoped to see if Christine had left a note. There was nothing on the tables or the pillow.

No big deal. She was in a rush, he assured himself. Last night still meant something to Christine. He knew it in the way she touched him, in her sighs of delight and her gasps of pleasure. The way she clung to him as if he was her rock, her shelter. It didn't mean she had to keep clinging once morning came.

It was probably better this way, he decided as he padded barefoot to his pile of clothes by the door. If they had tried to continue, his history would repeat itself. She would tire of his energy and his curiosity. He would start feeling trapped. What they shared was based on mutual desire. It was pure fantasy and that's how he wanted to remember it.

Travis reached down for the pile of clothes. He pushed aside his jeans and smiled when he saw Christine's bra had somehow gotten tangled up with the legs. He grabbed his jacket and retrieved his phone from the pocket. "Hello?" he said, his voice husky from sleep.

"Travis?" Aaron's loud voice pierced through his fog. "I've been trying to reach you. Where have you been?"

"I was asleep. How did the game go?"

"I won big," Aaron said triumphantly. "Was there any doubt?"

"Never," Travis lied. One of these days his friend was going to lose badly. Maybe lose the emerald that symbolized his good fortune.

"You should have seen Hoffmann when I won. The guy tried to cheat but he still lost. He really wants that emerald back."

"And I can't wait to get rid of this stone. Pitts and Underwood followed us everywhere."

"Us?" Aaron's voice squeaked. "The hot chick has been with you all this time?"

"Was there any doubt?" Travis teased as he went through the jacket pocket looking for the emerald. He must have moved it to his shirt pocket. "She just left for the airport. Where do you want to meet? We need to be careful because I don't think they've given up on the emerald just yet."

"Don't worry. I've been careful since I realized they searched my room," Aaron said. "I won't let my guard down."

"I can't wait to see the state of my hotel room," he muttered. Travis froze as alarm shot through him while he stared at the pile of clothes. Where was his shirt?

"How should I know?"

Travis winced. Did he say that out loud? "Sorry, just talking to myself," he said in a rush. "Let me call you back. I just got up." He disconnected the call before Aaron could reply.

Travis dropped to his knees and went through the pile of clothes again. His shirt was gone. There was no emerald. Travis searched around the floor. He spotted his wallet and quickly went through it. As far as he could tell, nothing was touched.

He tossed his wallet back onto the floor and tried to breathe as dread twisted inside him. This wasn't happening. What had happened to the emerald? Did Pitts and Underwood get it when they bumped into Christine? No, that couldn't have happened. He had checked and still had the emerald at the time. So who took it?

Something silky and delicate slithered through his fingers. He looked down with a frown as he saw the white bra in his hands.

Christine.

No. Travis immediately rejected that idea. Christine was a sweet and shy small-town girl looking for a wild weekend. She was not a jewel thief. She didn't have it in her to be a criminal mastermind.

Or had it all been pretend?

He tossed the bra to the ground and jumped to his feet. He needed to review the facts, Travis decided as he began to pace the small room. He was the one who had approached her. He was the one who'd made the first move.

And she was the one who took him to her hotel room and seduced him.

Seduced him? Travis rolled his eyes in self-disgust. She did more than that. She toyed with his emotions and made love to him. She knew what he had secretly craved. Her gentleness. Her sweetness. He hadn't considered that it was fake.

She was good. She disarmed him. Stripped him bare. Played him for a fool.

Travis strode to the window and pushed the curtains open. He stared unseeingly at the Las Vegas Strip as he considered the possibilities. Did she work with Pitts and Underwood? Or did she work alone?

All he knew was that Christine Pearson wasn't real. If that was even her real name. Anger burned inside him at the thought. Whoever she was, he wasn't going to let her get the best of him.

He was going to hunt her down, get back his friend's lucky charm and make her regret tangling with Travis Cain.

CHAPTER SEVEN

CHRISTINE WALKED UP to the front of her best friend's store in the center of Cedar Valley. The warm yellow wood siding and colorful hanging flowers were a welcome sight in the face of the incoming rain clouds. It had been only one day and Christine already missed Las Vegas.

She wasn't going to think about that, Christine decided as she carried the pile of clothes she had taken on vacation and walked to the dark green double doors. After visiting a place with the nickname Sin City, of course Cedar Valley would feel tiny and static. She needed to stop resisting the predictable rhythm of the town and accept it.

As she walked into Jill's dry-cleaning store, she heard the high-pitched bell above the door. Christine paused as it reminded her of the bells from the slot machines and the stunned expression on Travis's handsome face when she'd won.

Stop it, she fiercely warned herself. She needed to quit thinking about the weekend and start moving forward.

A short and curvy woman with a curly mop of copper hair stepped into the room. "Christine!" Jill said with a shriek. "I didn't expect to see you so soon. How was your trip?"

"Amazing," she said with a proud smile as she set the pile of clothes on the counter. "I raced in a Ferrari, I jumped out of a building and I won money at a slot machine."

Jill's mouth dropped open and she held up her hand. "Back

up. You jumped out of a building? That was on your dream list?"

"No, I hadn't planned on the jump."

Jill narrowed her eyes. "You mean you did it accidentally?"

"No!" she said with a laugh as she rested her arms on the old-fashioned counter. "They have this jump for tourists and I decided to do it."

"Good for you!" Jill reached over and gave a pat on her arm. "You didn't even stick to your list. You were just a wild woman, weren't you?"

"I wouldn't go that far." If she had been a wild woman, she would have had sex with Travis on the first night.

Jill tilted her head as she studied Christine's appearance. "There's something different about you. Did you get some color from the sun?"

Christine ducked her head. "I don't know. I haven't noticed."

"Oh, my God." Her friend jerked back and pointed a finger at her. "You had sex!"

"What?" She took a step back from the counter and looked around to make sure no one else was in the store. "How did you know? Is there a love bite I missed?" She dragged her fingers down her neck. "How obvious is it? Can I get rid of it before I go to work?"

Jill crossed her arms as she studied Christine. "No, you're good. There is no incriminating evidence on your body as far as I can tell."

She dropped her hands. "Then how did you figure it out?"

"You seem more relaxed," Jill said with a shrug. "So... how was it?"

Christine started to blush. "What happens in Vegas..."

"That good, huh?" Jill waggled her eyebrows. "Who was he? Did you get a name? Tell me you used protection. What does he look like? Where is he on the scale from one to ten? Ten, by the way, is a sex god."

"His name was Travis Cain." She hated how her voice caught when she said his name out loud. "He was incredibly hot and that's all I'm saying."

"Oh, come on," Jill insisted. "You have to give me some details. How wild was it?"

It wasn't wild. It was romantic and tender. Christine sighed. She couldn't do a one-night stand correctly. No, she had to get emotionally attached to the guy.

"Huh. I know that look. You liked him. A lot." Jill clucked her tongue. "Tell me you're not going to try for the long-distance relationship. Those things never work and, knowing you, you'd do all the traveling to keep it going."

That sounded like something she would do. Relationships and friendships had always been important to her. Too important. Unfortunately, she wasn't always top priority to her loved ones. "No. Travis doesn't stay in one place for long. He's all about freedom."

"Perfect," Jill said. "The last thing you need to do is enter another relationship. When I think of all you gave up to be with Darrell…"

"Don't worry, Jill. I learned my lesson." She had recognized the pattern after Darrell had dumped her. She had put aside her goal to see the world and focused on the people in her life. It wasn't just the men. It had also been her mother and some of her friends. She gave relationships her all but didn't get back the support.

It had been different in Vegas. She had enjoyed Travis's undivided attention, but it also made her uncomfortable. She was used to compromising, keeping quiet and letting someone else choose first. Travis wanted her to go after her interests with no apologies.

Did he do that hoping for a tumble in her bed? No, Christine decided. He would have given up on the first night. "This was a one-night stand," Christine told her friend, "and I'm not asking for more."

Jill pursed her lips as admiration danced in her eyes. "Ooh, look at you. So sophisticated."

"And late for work. I need to get there before Mrs. Lamb drops by for her weekly visit to her safe-deposit box." Christine groaned when she looked at the clock on the wall. "I feel like it's going to take a while to recover from this weekend."

"You're going to be fine," Jill said as she grabbed a basket and dumped the clothes in it. "I'll let you know when your clothes are ready. Hey, how much money did you win?"

"Not even a thousand," she admitted. Travis probably thought she was crazy to get excited over a few hundred bucks. He'll never know that she was more excited about adding him to her dream list.

"At least it's something," Jill said. "You can use the money for another wild weekend."

"Another one." For some reason, she wasn't excited about the idea. She hadn't considered where she wanted to go next. What was stopping her from taking another trip to Vegas?

"Well, yeah. See what you accomplished when you didn't have everyone in Cedar Valley looking over your shoulder?" Jill's eyebrows rose, hiding under the coppery curls. "You're not going to stop, are you?"

"Wouldn't think of it," she said as she left the store. Christine tried to ignore the pinch in her chest. Her Vegas weekend was a success because of Travis. She wouldn't be able to recapture the magic anywhere else with anyone else.

TRAVIS SLOWED HIS motorcycle on the street and looked around with a growing sense of horror. There were more trees than people, no cars parked on the cobblestone street and it was so quiet that he could hear the birds sing. He saw the hand-painted sign welcoming him to Cedar Valley, but it felt as if he had entered a different era.

There was no way Christine Pearson lived here, Travis decided as he easily found a spot to park his motorcycle. She may have been raised here or even passed through. She was too young, too curious about life, to have stayed.

The town was smaller than he had expected. Travis chuckled. It wasn't even a town. It was too small to be a village. He was surprised it was big enough to have earned a dot on the map.

He looked at the homes and businesses lined up on Main Street. This place once had money, a century or two ago. Now it was as quiet as a ghost town. But someone had to live here, considering how much effort had been expended to renovate the Victorian houses. They were well loved and freshly painted in colors that reminded him of Easter eggs.

This was an odd place for a jewel thief, Travis decided as he reluctantly got off his motorcycle and removed his helmet. Something about Cedar Valley made him tense, as if he knew he was going to make a false move. A mistake. He had traveled far and wide, from cosmopolitan cities to tribal lands. It took some time to learn the rituals and traditions, but here he had a very strong sense that he didn't belong.

It was genteel. Small-town Americana. As he strode down the sidewalk, he noticed the antiques store and teahouse. A carriage house had been converted into a small bookstore. The quaint post office had a small red-and-blue mailbox bolted to the wall. The brown building up ahead was the general store and he saw the white church steeple on the hill, peeking out above the fat, leafy trees.

"Good morning!"

Travis frowned when he heard the young male voice. Great, it was one of *those* towns. The kind of place where everyone knew you, your family history and your secrets. He never did well in places like this.

He turned around and nodded his head in acknowledgment to the man coming out of the bookstore. The stranger was pushing a cart of paperbacks on the small stone path.

"Are you lost?"

Travis heard the territorial edge underneath the friendly question and gave the man a closer look. He was a clean-cut kind of guy with a blue dress shirt and khaki pants. Bland, forgettable and enjoyed being the big fish in a small pond. "This is Cedar Valley, right?" Travis asked.

"Yes, it is. Sorry." His eyes narrowed with distaste at Travis's disreputable appearance. Apparently Cedar Valley had a dress code. Leather jackets and faded jeans didn't make the list. "Most of our visitors are older and come for our famous weekends."

"Famous weekends?"

The man stretched his arms out. "Cedar Valley is the Pacific Northwest weekend destination. We have a popular farmers' market and flower stand. The general store does a great picnic basket. If you're looking for a place to stay, we have a bed-and-breakfast, but it's always full on the weekends."

He really was in hell. "I'm looking for Christine Pearson."

"Christine?" The man thrust out his chin as if scenting trouble. Or competition. "How do you know her?"

"We're friends," Travis said, almost choking on the term. He had been infatuated with Christine, intrigued by her sweetness and innocence. And then she stole from him. He didn't know if she had made the most of an unexpected opportunity or if she had targeted him from the beginning.

"I'm Darrell." He watched Travis closely as they shook hands. The lines on Darrell's forehead deepened. "What? She never told you about me?"

"No," Travis replied brusquely and dropped Darrell's hand. Christine had mentioned everyone else from Cedar Valley but this guy. That had to be significant. "Do you know where I can find her?"

"Oh, sure. Christine's schedule never changes." Darrell glanced at his watch. "She would be working at the bank."

The bank? He should have guessed. It was a thief's dream job. "Where can I find it?"

"Just stay on Main Street. The bank is the only brick building in town. If you pass the gazebo in the town's square, you've gone too far."

A gazebo. He should have known. This place was a freaking nightmare. Once he confronted Christine and got the emerald back, he was leaving like a bat out of hell.

AT EXACTLY TEN O'CLOCK, Christine rose from her desk and left her glassed-in office. She walked out to the lobby of the Cedar Valley Bank. There were no customers and the two bank tellers were chatting with each other. Christine nodded at Harold, the old security guard, as Faye Lamb and her daughter, Bonnie, walked through the front door.

She could hear Faye and Bonnie bickering. Bonnie was in her late forties and always wore a baseball cap and colorful workout clothes. Faye was in her seventies and never left the house without her jewelry and makeup on. And, since the death of her husband, Faye wore only black. The mother and daughter were very different, but their love and affection for each other were apparent.

Christine had always felt she and Bonnie had something in common. Like Bonnie, Christine had put her life on hold when her father had left and her mother had been too grief-stricken to cope. Christine was glad her mother eventually found a second chance at love and left Cedar Valley to start a new life. She just wished she hadn't focused so much on others and had done something for herself during those years.

"Christine!" Faye Lamb said as she shuffled across the lobby, her black heels clacking on the marble floor. "It's good to see you. How was your vacation?"

She forgot that everyone knew she had been out of town. "It was wonderful," Christine said with a warm smile as she greeted Faye with a gentle handshake. The older woman was fragile and wore heavy, sharp rings and bracelets.

"You won't believe what happened," Faye said with a smile. "My son is coming for a visit."

"Really?" She barely remembered Todd, but she had heard the stories. He had a talent for finding trouble. She glanced at Bonnie for confirmation and the woman nodded. "Todd hasn't been back home for ages. What's the occasion?"

"He hasn't said," Bonnie informed Christine. "Knowing Todd, it'll be a short visit."

"It sounds as if you'll want to break out the good jewelry," Christine said.

"That's what I was thinking," Faye said as they slowly walked to the door that led to the safe-deposit boxes. "This calls for the pearls."

Christine remembered the stunning pearl necklace and automatically reached up to brush her hand along the fake pearls she wore every day to work. She'd bought the necklace years ago so she would feel older and more sophisticated at the office.

"You know," Faye said, "my dearly departed Stanley gave me the necklace when Todd was born."

"I thought he gave you that bracelet to celebrate Todd's birth." Christine pointed at the thick gold chain bracelet that Faye always wore. The woman enjoyed changing her jewelry on a weekly basis, but the bracelet never left her wrist.

"No, no, no." Faye waved her hand and the gold flashed warmly under the ceiling lights. "The bracelet was when we found out I was pregnant."

"That's right. Now I remember." Christine liked this part of her job. She wanted to hear the stories about the family heirlooms or a person's most valued possession. She wanted to see a customer's eyes light up when they dreamed about retirement or the possibilities of their first home.

"It's only right that I give both to Todd when he comes over," Faye said softly.

Christine paused as she waved another employee to come over to assist them. "I beg your pardon?"

"My mother thinks Todd would appreciate the family heirlooms." Bonnie shook her head wearily. "She wants him to present them to his fiancée on a special occasion. What fiancée is he on now? Number eight?"

"Hush, now," Faye said. "It took Todd some time to find his true love. That necklace will seal the deal. Mark my words."

"Here is Laurie to help you with the box," Christine said, even though Faye and Bonnie were familiar with the procedure. "Please let me know if you need anything."

As Christine returned to her office, she thought about the jewelry that dear departed Stanley had given his wife. The pieces were old, heavy and didn't fit the current styles, but Christine thought the ritual had been sweet and romantic. Faye relived the memories every time she wore one of Stanley's gifts.

Christine was about to sit down at her desk when she heard the unfamiliar throaty growl of a motorcycle. That was odd. No one in Cedar Valley had a motorcycle.

She glanced out the window as she saw the rider turn into the parking lot. He wore a black motorcycle jacket, faded jeans and boots and a black helmet. There was something familiar about the lean, muscular body. She wondered who'd bought a bike over the weekend. She didn't remember anyone coming in asking for a loan.

As the man parked in front of the bank and removed the helmet, Christine went still. That looked like Travis Cain. She blinked. The same high cheekbones and angular jaw.

She blinked again and stared at his harsh features. Her skin went hot and then cold. Her heart leaped in her chest and she gasped.

Oh, no. That *was* Travis Cain. What was he doing here?

There was only one answer. He was here to see her. Christine looked at her dull brown dress and her hands automatically went to her tight braid. *Oh, no, no, no.* She dropped to her knees and hid from the window. She couldn't let this happen.

The panic pulsed in her body as she looked for an escape. She had no second door. The walls were glass. There wasn't another exit.

She needed to make a run for it. Christine was about to stand when she heard the heavy footsteps on the marble floor.

"Good morning, sir," Laurie said with a tinge of curiosity. "How can I help you?"

"I'm here for Christine Pearson."

Christine shivered when she heard Travis's voice. It was husky and confident. The man didn't need to raise his voice. He always gained attention the moment he stepped into a room.

"She should be in her office," Laurie said. "I'll take you there."

CHAPTER EIGHT

CHRISTINE DOVE UNDER her desk. She winced and gritted her teeth when her knee bumped against the sharp edge of a drawer. She tried not to make a sound as she curled her body tight. Resting her forehead against her stinging knee, she closed her eyes. Her pulse was racing, her heart pounding in her ears, as she listened to Laurie's squeaky flat shoes get closer.

"Christine?" Laurie's voice grew louder as she stepped into the small office. "Huh, that's strange. I could have sworn she was here."

Christine pressed her lips together and prayed Laurie wouldn't investigate and walk around the desk. The older woman would immediately call her out. Laurie wouldn't understand that she was hiding from Travis until it was too late.

"She must have just stepped out," Laurie continued. "Perhaps I could help you?"

"I'm not a customer," Travis said. Christine's heart did a slow, funny flip at the sound of his voice. "I'm here on personal business."

"Really?"

Christine scrunched up her face at Laurie's intrigued tone. The woman was hardworking and helpful, but her favorite pastime was gossiping. She could probably get information out of a hardened criminal with a carefully placed question and a cookie.

She didn't want Travis talking to Laurie. Christine was

tempted to jump out from under the desk just to keep Laurie and Travis apart. Maybe she could cause a distraction. Christine looked around the room as the anxiety pulsed inside her. She had nothing.

Perhaps she didn't have anything to worry about. Travis was discreet. He was friendly but private. He didn't reveal a lot about himself.

She wasn't sure why she hadn't noticed that before. He'd entertain her with stories about his travels, but he was hesitant to answer any personal questions. She knew that he had risked death while snowboarding in Alaska, but she didn't know where he was born. She was sure he would respond in the same manner to Laurie's pointed questions.

"I'm sure Christine will be back shortly," Laurie said. "Would you like a cup of coffee while you wait?"

Don't do it! Tell her you'll come back, Christine thought. She needed Travis to leave so she could get out of here. She needed time to come up with a plan for how she would act when she came face-to-face with her one-night stand.

"Thank you."

"Are you from around here?" Laurie asked. "What did you say your family name was?"

"I'm Travis Cain, and no, this is my first time in Cedar Valley."

Christine shook her head. Why was Travis giving out unsolicited information? He was making it too easy for Laurie. The man knew how to deflect personal questions. He did it during her Vegas weekend. Did he want to hide something from me or was Laurie just that good at interrogation?

"I knew you didn't look familiar," Laurie said, her voice fading as they went closer to the front door, where the complimentary drinks were served. "So how do you know Christine?"

Christine strained to listen to Travis's reply but all she heard was the timbre of his deep voice. Her stomach twisted as she imagined how he replied. *I met her while she was gambling away her life's savings.... I spent the weekend with her in bed....* She was going to be the talk of the town before lunchtime.

She couldn't let that happen. She had spent the past ten years building a reputation. Christine Pearson was no longer the dreamer who didn't understand reality. She now was the woman who knew how to make dreams happen for others. She was the advocate for her friends and neighbors and got to live the dream through them. She was the fairy godmother she'd never had. She wasn't going to let one wild weekend ruin that.

She had to do something, but she needed help. Christine carefully uncurled herself from under the desk and reached for the bottom drawer. She hissed as the metal rubbed against metal. She grabbed her purse and found her cell phone. Christine hunched her shoulders and returned to the safe haven under her desk as she speed-dialed her friend.

"Jill's Dry Cleaning."

"Jill?" she whispered fiercely and then paused. As far as she could tell, no one heard her in the quiet bank. "It's Christine. I need your help."

"You got it." Jill's voice dropped low. "Why are we whispering?"

"Travis just showed up at the bank." She didn't know how Jill was going to handle the news. Neither of them had ever had a man follow them to the ends of the earth. Or Cedar Valley, which sometimes felt like the farthest edge of civilization. Would Jill worry or cheer her on? She hoped it would be brief because it was getting extremely uncomfortable under this desk.

"Travis?" Jill said the name as if she was testing it out on her tongue. "Who's Travis? Wait, wasn't your one-night stand named Travis?"

"Yes, that's the guy. Travis Cain. He drove up to the bank on a motorcycle and is talking to Laurie."

"Uh-oh. Of all the people to meet in Cedar Valley. She's going to find out everything you did in Vegas and tell everyone," Jill predicted. "Then the whole town is going to question your judgment. Jumping out of a building is one thing, but gambling? And a one-night stand with a stranger? They aren't going to trust you with their money."

"I know." Christine rubbed her hand over her face as she considered the worst-case scenario. Any lack of faith and she could lose her job. "Travis is hanging around waiting for me to return."

"Where are you?"

"I hit the floor the minute I saw him," she admitted. "And now I'm hiding under my desk. I can't escape without anyone noticing."

"This guy followed you from Vegas? Should I be concerned?"

Christine jerked in surprise. "No, Travis isn't a stalker. I didn't get any creepy vibes from him. He never made me uncomfortable. In fact, I was the one who was in charge of this fling. I took *him* to bed."

"I'll take your word for it," Jill said. "But how did he know where you live?"

"I don't know." Christine shook her head and sighed. "I may have mentioned Cedar Valley once or twice."

"Christine! The next time I see you, we will discuss what you can and cannot reveal when you have sex with a stranger."

"I really don't think this situation will come up again," Christine whispered fiercely and clapped her hand over mouth. She looked from side to side as she listened for anyone approaching her office. "Tell me how to get out of this."

Jill clucked her tongue. "There is only one thing you can do. You need to suck it up, buttercup."

Christine swallowed a groan as she heard her friend give the usual advice. "I was really afraid you would say that."

"Get out from under the desk," Jill told her, "look him

in the eye and tell him that you are a married woman with seven children."

"Jill!" She covered her mouth again as a laugh threatened to escape. There was no way she could tell a lie like that.

"You have a better idea?"

"I don't want to see him." That wasn't true. She wanted to see Travis again. Wrap her arms around him and claim a kiss. Feel the sizzle in her veins and the throb of pleasure as he awakened her body. But she needed to do it on her terms. She glanced down at her brown shift dress and sensible shoes. "You saw how I looked this morning."

"What was wrong with your appearance? It's a clean, tailored look. Very proper and ladylike."

"That's the problem." Christine leaned her head against her desk and winced from the unyielding metal. "He's under the impression that I'm a sexy and exciting woman."

"You are a sexy and exciting woman," Jill insisted.

Christine smiled. Her friend was loyal but wrong. "I'm not wearing strapless dresses and high heels day after day. I'm not having all-night sex in my real life."

"Well, no wonder he followed you from Vegas," Jill muttered. "What exactly did you do during the sex marathons?"

"Nothing!" She didn't do anything that would have him chasing her for more. That was what made this so confusing. "I just don't get it."

"Okay, what do you want to do?"

Christine held her hands out as she considered her options. "I got a plan. I need you to come over here and smuggle in a little black dress and some stiletto heels."

"Right," Jill said in a drawl. "Like that's not going to cause a scene. Your coworkers are so used to you walking around the bank in evening wear."

Her friend was right. If she sexed up her appearance, it would create more gossip. But it would hurt to approach Travis now and watch the desire in his eyes fizzle. "I can't let him see me like this."

"Why not? It's the real you."

She tilted her foot and looked at her shoe. They were dowdy but comfortable. Just like every other pair of shoes in her closet. "He wouldn't be interested in the real me."

"Now I'm confused. Do you want him here or not?"

Christine sighed. "I want to see him again, but not like this. Not in my natural habitat. He's going to expect a swan and find a colorless, boring duck. My pride is at stake here."

"If he's that kind of guy, you don't want him in the first place."

"I know. I just wish…" Christine bit her tongue before she voiced her deepest desire. She wanted Travis to think she was so fascinating that he couldn't believe his luck that he was with her. She wished she could have one person in this world think she was special. Even if it was a lie.

"You need me to come over there and run interference?" Jill offered. "I can cause a distraction while you crawl out the window."

"Thanks for the offer," Christine said as she reluctantly withdrew from her hiding place. "But that didn't work in high school, and I don't think it's going to work now."

"What are you going to do?"

"The only thing I can do. I'm going to show Travis the real me. He'll walk out of here and I'll have a chance to contain the gossip. No one will know about my secret weekend."

"It's for the best," Jill assured her.

Christine knew that, but her heart wasn't in it. This had been her one chance to be a man's fantasy. Now that moment was gone.

TRAVIS TOOK A SIP of coffee and cast a quick glance at Christine's office. She was still hiding under the desk. Did she really think he wouldn't have noticed? The desk was on short legs and he had seen her feet.

The anger swirling inside him was cold and hard. He wanted to walk around the desk and crouch down, surround and trap her until she handed over the emerald. But his instincts told him to play dumb. Pretend the way she was pretending. He had struggled to remain standing in the doorway, but he trusted his instincts more than the hurt and anger that tore him up inside.

"You're telling me she raced a sports car?" Laurie said slowly. "Our Christine Pearson?"

Travis turned to face Laurie. She had a motherly quality about her. Her salt-and-pepper hair swung just below her chin. Her blue eyes sparkled with interest and concern behind the cat-eye glasses. She wore a thin green cardigan over a floral-print dress. Laurie appeared unassuming, but he wasn't going to lower his guard.

"She was a natural," Travis said with a smile. He admired Laurie's ability to elicit information from him. He knew how to sidestep the questions. It was a technique he had learned while growing up. His grandmother wouldn't leave the house and at times her fears were so great, she wouldn't let him out, either. It was easier to make up stories and excuses than to reveal the truth.

But he wanted to know more about Christine and an incurable gossip was the best source. He had to give a little to receive something in return. Laurie wanted information, but her true mission was spreading it around. She was the expert on everyone in Cedar Valley and wanted him to know it. "You sound surprised," he said. "Christine is a speed demon."

"I shouldn't be surprised," Laurie said with a frown. "Christine used to be like that. She was the kind of girl who climbed the water tower because it was the tallest structure in the area. Stood on her bike as if it was a surfboard and rode down the hill at full speed. But that changed once her dad ran out and she became the head of the household."

Travis didn't want to think of Christine as a carefree girl who had to grow up fast, but he instantly imagined a young woman trying to make ends meet. She would dress in clothes that were too old for her and take the role of caregiver seriously. A little too seriously.

He didn't want to think about her navigating the adult world without any guidance. He needed to remember that she was a thief. Christine Pearson stole his friend's emerald. Travis clenched his teeth as he recalled Aaron's face when he had to admit he'd lost the stone. He had failed his friend— one of the few people in this world who mattered to him— and he had to make things right. He wasn't going to find the emerald if he fell for Christine's innocent act.

"What else did she do in Vegas?" Laurie asked.

"She was very interested in extreme sports," Travis said, hoping his voice carried to Christine's office. "The bigger the risk the better."

"Christine?" Laurie said in a squawk. "Are you sure we're talking about the same person? You should see her investment portfolio. It's about as low-risk as you can get."

"She did a sky jump," Travis revealed. He set his coffee cup down and reached for his cell phone. "I think I have a picture somewhere on my phone."

Laurie chuckled and rubbed her hands together. "Oh, I wish Darrell could see this."

Travis glanced up sharply at the older woman. "Her ex-boyfriend? Why?"

"Don't worry about him, sweetie." She gave him a knowing look and patted him on the arm. "There is no competition. That is over and done with. She would never take him back after how he humiliated her."

Travis glanced at Christine's empty office. He knew she was shy and blushed easily. She didn't know how to attract attention, but did she avoid it because of an embarrassing experience? "What do you mean?"

"He had one too many beers at the bar one night," Laurie said in a confiding tone, "and announced to the whole town that he was breaking up with her because he found her boring."

"Christine?" Travis's eyes widened in surprise. The woman had a thirst for adventure and an interest in everything. She couldn't shake loose her cautious nature, but her excuses to avoid any risk were just as entertaining as watching her explore the world around her.

"That's what he said," Laurie said with a cluck of her tongue. "Especially in bed."

His mouth dropped open. "Say what?" Christine had been magical and mind-blowing in bed. Nothing she did had been mechanical or predictable. She gave from the heart and had made their one night memorable.

"Hmm…you don't agree?" Her blue eyes danced with triumph. "Good to know."

Travis clipped his jaw shut. Damn, this woman was good. He wanted to shake Christine out of her hiding place with a few mentions about Vegas, but he wasn't going to discuss that night. She may have had an ulterior motive taking him to bed, but it meant something to him. He wasn't going to share that moment with anyone else.

"How did Christine respond?" he asked. Most women he knew would retaliate.

"Christine didn't make a scene. She handled it with grace, just as we knew she would," Laurie said with a hint of admiration. "Now I wonder if she went to Vegas to let her hair down. Prove to herself that he was wrong."

Was that also why she took the emerald? Did she need to do something extreme, something illegal, to show that her ex-boyfriend was wrong about her? That made more sense to him than the other motives he had considered.

"Travis?" Christine's unsteady voice echoed in the lobby. "I thought I heard you."

Travis's breath hitched in his throat when he saw Christine in the lobby. His heart began to pound as she walked toward him. Her brown eyes seemed bigger and her features appeared more delicate. The simple brown dress highlighted her pale skin and feminine body. Her movements were innately sensual. She didn't need high heels to show off her incredible legs.

Christine had a determined smile on her face as she clutched her cell phone as if it was her lifeline. He knew she wanted to take control of this reunion and get him out of here. In the most ladylike fashion, of course, because that was what people expected.

Not if he could help it. "Christine." He held his arms out wide.

Her smile took a dip as she stood in front of him. "What are you doing here?"

"You know why I'm here."

"No…" She gave a cautious look at Laurie, who showed no interest in leaving them alone. "No, I don't."

So that was how she was going to play it. Innocent until the very end. He could play this game, too. Expose her lies and her true self to her friends.

He stepped forward and gathered her in his arms. "I missed you," he admitted in a growl. "I missed this."

Her body went rigid in his embrace. "I don't understand."

"You left so quickly yesterday morning," he complained. "Snuck away like a *thief*."

"Um…Travis?" She looked from side to side as her cheeks turned red. "What has gotten into you?"

He didn't know. He meant to pretend he was a devoted lover, but it felt too real. He found the pull irresistible. Travis bent his head and claimed her mouth. Heat exploded between them as she parted her lips. He darted his tongue into her mouth, desperate for another taste of her.

He broke away when he realized he was getting into dangerous territory. She had a hold on him that he didn't understand and didn't want to break. "I'm not ready to let you go," he said gruffly.

Christine carefully stepped out of his embrace and gestured to the door. "Why don't we step outside and discuss this?"

"As you wish." He gave a sharp nod. "I'll follow you anywhere."

CHAPTER NINE

CHRISTINE SCANNED THE area when they stepped outside the bank. No one was around, but she knew her coworkers were watching her from the windows. She was tempted to find a private spot, but that was asking for trouble. Especially after that kiss.

She brushed her fingertips against her mouth. She wanted to kiss Travis so much that her lips stung with need. The instant attraction they had shared in Vegas had been exciting and new. Now it was inconvenient.

And the flare of desire in his eyes didn't make sense. She didn't turn heads when she walked through town. Why would Travis watch her as if he knew exactly what she looked like underneath?

"Okay, Travis," she said as she strolled to a tree with low branches next to the parking lot. "What is really going on?"

"You tell me."

She gave him a quick glance when she heard his sharp tone. She saw his harsh features and felt his hot gaze. She had never seen him this intense. "I don't understand. Is this some kind of joke?"

"Believe me," he said in a low voice, "I've never been more serious."

"Why me?" She turned and leaned against the tree trunk, then looked up to meet his gaze. "You had your choice of women in Vegas."

He gave her a curious look. "And I chose you. The question is why did you choose me?"

"Are you kidding?" she asked. Travis was everything she admired in a man. He was a mix of strength and gentleness, of knowledge and action. When she was in his arms, she felt safe to break out of her comfort zone.

"Why did you?" he asked. "I really want to know."

"Travis, what we had was fun." She didn't like that description; it made her time in Vegas sound trivial. That weekend changed her. Travis changed her. "But I am not the kind of woman men pursue."

He tilted his head. "What are you talking about?"

Wasn't it already glaringly obvious? Christine curled her hand tighter against her cell phone and the device bit into her palm. She had never been mysterious or stunning. She didn't attract male attention.

She didn't mind it. At least, that's what she told herself. She had other things to offer in a relationship. She was the caregiver, the cheering section. But that wasn't enough to hold a man, apparently. When Darrell dumped her because she wasn't exciting enough, it had been a wake-up call.

But she still wasn't stunning or mysterious. She could dress the part of the femme fatale, but she was still too cautious to fulfill what the sexy shoes promised.

"You wouldn't have noticed me in the casino if I had dressed like this," Christine said as she gestured at her dress.

Travis flattened his hand on the tree trunk above her. "You wouldn't have noticed me if I hadn't approached you."

"Don't be so sure." Her dream list didn't include sex with a tall, dark and gorgeous man, but that didn't mean she wouldn't have noticed Travis.

He leaned in. "Would you have done something about it?"

Her world was growing smaller as Travis filled her senses. She pressed her spine against the rough bark. "Depends on how brave I felt at the time."

"How brave do you feel now?" he asked. He raised his other hand and caressed her cheek. She trembled from the soft touch. "We're in your territory now and you know that I came all this way to find you."

"It's different," she insisted hoarsely. "This isn't Vegas. I have to be on my best behavior."

Her phone chimed. She glanced at the text from Jill. *He kissed you?* Christine closed her eyes and groaned. Gossip traveled fast in this town.

"Does your best behavior include hiding under a desk?" Travis asked as his hand rested against the fluttering pulse at the base of her throat.

She opened her eyes wide as the embarrassment gripped her. She could barely breathe. "What?" Her voice sounded strangled as heat scorched her skin.

"Just now?" He gestured at the bank building. "There is no other door to your office. You were under the desk, weren't you?"

"Okay, yes." Christine tossed her hands in the air in defeat. She should have known she was no match for Travis Cain. He saw everything. And why wouldn't he? She was no different from the countless women who threw themselves at his feet. "You caught me. I should have expected that. I panicked when I saw you."

His eyes darkened. "Why?"

"I didn't want you to see me," she said in a harsh whisper. "Not like this."

Travis's hand drifted down the side of her body, grazing her breast. "Like how?" he asked.

"I'm not a woman of action, but I want to be. I went to Vegas and pretended to be someone else. A bolder version of myself...." Her voice trailed off as she became very aware of Travis's hand spanning her waist. "But I wasn't that brazen after all."

His hand skimmed her hip. "I don't understand."

"I'm just a small-town girl," she admitted. "My days are filled with my job and my friends. That's it. I haven't traveled around the world. I don't even have a passport."

"Then how…" His fingers flexed against her hip as he looked around the bank. "This doesn't make sense."

"I lied because I didn't think the real me would interest you. I still don't." She heard the chime of her cell phone. She squeezed the phone in her hand and ignored it.

"So the bucket list was a lie, too?"

"No, that was the truth. There really is one." *Unfortunately,* she thought with a twist of her lips. She wished she had never found it. It only reminded her of time wasted. Of dreams unfulfilled.

"How do I know it wasn't some pickup line?" he asked. "A clever way to keep me at your side. I never saw the list. I was taking your word for it."

If only she was that clever when it came to luring men. "I didn't have it with me because I had it memorized."

"Anything else you'd like to confess?"

"Didn't you hear me? The list is true. It's a real thing," she insisted. "My friend Jill has seen it. I don't go waving it around to people because it's not something to brag about. I only have two things checked off."

"Wait a second." He let go of her waist and placed his hand on the tree trunk, trapping her. "You told me you wrote it when you were eighteen. That you had a hundred items on the list."

She felt a wave of prickly heat crawl up her neck. "Yes," she muttered.

"You only accomplished two things in ten years? That can't be true."

She wanted to say it was because she was confined here in Cedar Valley. That she couldn't take a risk with her neighbors watching, waiting for her to fail. But she knew that was no longer true. That had been an excuse.

"I wanted to do all those things but life got in the way," she said dully. "Whenever I wanted to try something, my plans fell apart. If I raised the money for a trip, I would suddenly have to use that money for emergency home repairs."

"You're not the type to give up at the first sign of failure."

"I'm not," she said with a small smile, pleased that he recognized that about her. "But after a series of setbacks and disappointments, I thought I'd take a break. The crazy thing is that I'm much better at helping my friends and family achieve *their* dreams. I'm good at it. I thought it would be good practice until it was my turn."

"But your turn never happened," Travis guessed. "Until last weekend when you decided it was your time. That's why you were in Vegas. No other reason?"

She shrugged. "Why else would I be there alone?"

Travis peered into her eyes. What could he see? Christine wondered. Could he tell that her life was built more on disappointments than achievements? That nothing came easy for her? She would read every article on setting goals and still come up short. There was a time when she used to think something was wrong with her. Why else did some people get everything they wanted and she was still waiting for a break?

"What two things did you cross off?" he asked suddenly. "I know one of them was to win money."

Christine winced. Oh, why did he have to catch that part of the confession? "I decided that if I crossed one item off, I could add one," she explained.

"The last thing you did in Vegas was win money. After that…."

She fought to meet his gaze. "After that…was you."

Christine saw the light of surprise in his eyes. The sharp, angular features in his face softened. The edge of his mouth tilted up as he gave her a confident, sexy smile.

She crossed her arms and glared at Travis. "Shut up. I don't want to hear it."

His smile grew wider. "I didn't say a word."

"You don't have to." She had some crazy dreams on that list and now she'd given him the biggest ego boost.

"Hey, why are you glaring at me?" he said with a laugh. "You're the one who added a one-night stand on your list."

"No, I added you," she corrected him. "And I crossed you off the list."

His smile disappeared. "Was that why you slept with me? Because of some list?"

"If I was desperate to check something off my list, I would have added sky jumping or driving a Ferrari," she said. "I could have added anything on my list and I wanted you. I wanted you the moment I saw you, but I wasn't going to get distracted.

"I wanted you more than anything else Vegas had to offer."

"And now that you've had me, you've crossed me off your bucket list and you no longer have any interest in me. Is that it?"

I wish. Instead of getting Travis Cain out of her system, she realized she wanted him more than ever. "No, that's not it at all. I know that Cedar Valley will bore you. I'm just saving you some time."

"Christine, you had my full attention the moment you stepped into that casino. Nothing's going to change that."

His declaration warmed her. Travis might believe what he was saying, but she knew it wasn't going to last. "Big words for a man who doesn't believe in staying in one place for long," she murmured. "Don't say I didn't warn you."

SHE WAS GOOD. Travis watched Christine closely. She was selling this little innocent small-town girl routine. For a moment he believed it. He wanted Christine to be exactly what he first thought—a mix of sweet and spice.

Was it possible that she could just be a hardworking woman who hadn't had a chance to go after her dreams? And that emerald could bring in enough money that she could leave this tiny town and live out her craziest, most expensive fantasies?

He wished Christine wasn't the thief, but he had to face facts. She was the only person who could have stolen the emerald. His suspicions were confirmed when she hid from him. Only a guilty person would panic.

She'd recovered quickly. It made him wonder how often she found herself confronted by the victim of her crimes. She said she was hiding because of how she was dressed? That made no sense. She was beautiful and sensual and no clothes could hide that.

"Oh, great. I just saw my neighbor walk by," she muttered. "She doesn't come to the bank on Mondays. She must have heard about your public display of affection in the lobby."

"You were with me every step of the way," he said with deep satisfaction. This woman who was way out of his league put him on her bucket list. Her Vegas to-do list. He couldn't help but smile.

"Hello, Rhonda," Christine said. Travis watched Christine give a friendly wave at a young woman with a pixie cut and a long, flowing dress. "Looks like it's going to storm today."

"Good morning, Christine," Rhonda called back as she strolled to the bank's main entrance. "I see you brought a souvenir back from Vegas."

Christine slumped against the tree trunk and groaned. "Do you see what you started?" she asked Travis.

"And that's when I'm on my best behavior," Travis replied. It was time for her to figure out how much trouble he could cause.

"They are going to think that I've lost my mind." She covered her face with her hands. "They won't believe it was a phase and I'm too young to be having a midlife crisis."

"They'll think it was a knee-jerk response to how Darrell broke up with you." That would explain her Vegas weekend. He was beginning to think this was Christine's motive for taking the emerald. She was probably regretting taking the gem and didn't know what to do to fix the situation. That sounded more like the Christine he knew.

Christine's shoulders went rigid and her hands slowly dragged down her cheeks as she stared at him. "How did you know about that?"

He shrugged. "I heard things."

She spread her arms out wide. "You've only been in town for five minutes!"

"I met Darrell the moment I drove past the welcome sign." How could someone with Christine's wild streak be attracted to such a bland guy? "Really, Christine? What were you thinking?"

"And you think I'm better matched with you? Remember that the woman you met in Vegas was the fake me. The pretend Christine."

Travis didn't think so. He believed that he'd seen the real Christine in Vegas. The pretend one was standing before him now. "I'll soon find out."

Christine narrowed her eyes. "How are you going to do that?"

"I saw a bed-and-breakfast just off Main Street. I'm going to reserve a room." He suspected the place would be frilly and floral. It was going to be torture.

"You're staying there?" Christine started to shake her head. "You're going to hate it. The woman who runs it has so many rules. You're going to get kicked out before you unpack."

"Where else can I stay? Unless you're inviting me to your place," he teased.

Her eyelashes fluttered and she bit her bottom lip. "It's a mess."

Travis's stomach clenched when he saw the sparkle in Christine's eyes. She was considering having him stay? He thought he was the only one who wanted to continue what they had started. "I like messy."

"It's small," she warned him.

"Sounds cozy." Maybe too cozy. If he wasn't careful, he was going to prowl around like a caged animal. Was that what Christine was counting on?

"People will talk." She glanced around the parking lot.

"They're already talking," he pointed out. "You could deny we're involved, but no one would believe you."

Christine lowered her gaze and he knew she wasn't going to invite him. Something was holding her back. Was the emerald in her home?

"I'm sorry, Travis. I can't have you stay at my place. Not yet."

"It's okay. I understand." He pressed his hands against the tree trunk and leaned into her. Travis brushed his mouth against her lips. He did it again and again. He ached to hold Christine until he could feel her heart beating against him. Until their breathing became one.

Christine clasped her hands against his jaw and claimed his lips. She thrust her tongue into his mouth and explored him. He tasted her passion and her need. Her groan reverberated deep in her chest. Desire flared between them, burning bright, as the kiss grew stronger. Harder.

He pulled away before he got in too deep, but he couldn't break the connection. Their lips clung as his forehead rested against hers.

"Why'd you stop?" she whispered.

"If I don't stop now I'll take you against this tree." Christine Pearson wanted him. The seduction in Vegas hadn't been faked. He should be thrilled, but it just added another problem for him. This woman had stolen his friend's emerald and was lying about it, but he still couldn't keep his hands off her.

Christine suddenly ducked under his arm. Her movements were jerky and she didn't look at him. "I have to go back to work."

He reached for her hand and stopped her. "Stay with me," he urged.

"Travis, this is a really bad idea."

She was right. It was a bad idea. He didn't know why he felt this way or why he needed to hold on to her. There was something about Christine that he couldn't get enough of.

"I'm going to be honest. I'm not interested in a relationship," she said. "There are so many things I want to do and I need to make up for lost time."

"Then let me help you. Look at what you did in Vegas."

"Thanks, but I can't," she said with a smile. "I went to Vegas because I couldn't do those things here."

"Christine, you can do anything you want here. You just have to be smart about it."

She hesitated and then shook her head as if to clear his advice from her mind. "You're a bad influence."

"I'll show you everything I know," he promised. It could be fun. Addicting. He needed to be very careful or the student would overpower the master.

"Okay, fine. I would love to see how your mind works."

A chill swept through him. "What are you talking about?"

"You offered and I accepted," she said as she walked back to the bank. "Ready or not, I'm going to find out everything about you."

CHAPTER TEN

"THE PEOPLE IN Cedar Valley sure like to walk," Travis said as he took a sip from his beer bottle and leaned back on Christine's porch swing. It creaked as it gently moved back and forth. He gave a nod to a young couple in bright yellow raincoats as they strolled hand in hand down the sidewalk in the pouring rain. The two looked like they belonged in a sappy romantic musical. "I didn't see anyone when I first arrived and now I feel like I've seen the whole town strolling down your street."

"You are the talk of Cedar Valley," Christine said, sitting next to him. She had changed out of the brown dress and wore a thin red blouse and dark jeans. Her hair was loose and fell past her shoulders, but his gaze kept going to her bare feet. He hadn't expected her to go barefoot in front of him. It felt like an act of trust, but he knew he was reading too much into it.

"Why are people talking about me?" he asked. "I didn't do anything. Yet."

"Doesn't matter." She waved at the couple and they waved back. "They want to see what you look like. If we weren't sitting out on my porch, they would find an excuse to ring my front door."

"And here I thought we were sitting here because you wanted to show me off," he teased. He was surprised that she had invited him to her house, but he didn't get past the front door.

He had to find a way to get into the house. He needed a

chance to discover where she was hiding the emerald. Unless she had it in a safe-deposit box. His stomach twisted with dread at that possibility. He would never get it back if that was the case.

He looked around the screened-in porch again. It was vibrant but relaxing. He could stay here for hours. "This is your favorite spot at home, isn't it?"

She gave him a sharp look. "How did you know that?"

"It's you." From the small glimpse he had of her home, it had minimal furnishings and very few trinkets or pictures. The porch, however, was an explosion of color from the hunter-green floor to the printed throw pillows. There were plants in the corner and a shelf that held books and a stereo system.

"My parents never used the porch so I claimed it for myself. I wasn't stuck inside, but I wasn't out in the wild, either. It was a compromise."

"Do you have your bucket list here?" he asked, glancing at the shelf. He didn't see a box or a container that would store paper. Or an emerald. Chances were the stolen gem was where she kept her valuables. That bucket list was important to her. The emerald would be near it.

"You are obsessed with that list!" Christine said. "I swear there is one."

He reached over and splayed his hand on her denim-covered leg. "Then tell me one thing on the list you don't want people to know about."

She scoffed at his suggestion. "Why would I tell you that?"

"I want to know what you wanted when you were eighteen that you don't want now."

"There are actually a lot of things on that list that I don't think I'll do," she said as she gave him a thoughtful look. "I wanted to build my dream home. That was number twelve. It was going to be glamorous and in a big city. I had always felt cramped in this house and my dream home would have been a showcase for all the things I picked up on my travels."

Travis couldn't picture Christine in a big city, but she was someone who had souvenirs and scrapbooks. "And now?"

"I want to stay here. I'm lucky I don't have a mortgage and I want to spend my time and money on something else. But it's more than that. I always felt safe here. I can't replace that."

Her comment reminded him of his grandmother. The woman only felt safe at home until it got to the point that she couldn't leave the house. "You wouldn't sell it so you could go on a big adventure?"

"No. I need to know this is here for me. This is my home base. There were times when I struggled to keep it for my mother and me. I'm glad I fought through those moments." She took a sip of her beer and sighed. "What about you?"

He frowned. "What about me?"

"What did you want at eighteen?"

"I didn't want to turn out like my grandmother." The words slipped from his mouth before he thought about it. He winced. Why did he tell her that? That was something he would never admit, even to himself.

"I don't understand," Christine said softly.

"My grandmother raised me," Travis explained tersely. "She had a lot of phobias that got in the way of living. By the time I was a teenager, she wouldn't leave the house. Fear ruled her life and I didn't want to live like that."

The silence stretched between them as the porch swing creaked back and forth. Travis clenched his teeth. Why didn't he say something else? Why didn't he lie?

"What do you want now?" she asked.

He was thirty-one now but his goal had never changed. He had heard stories about his grandmother when she was younger. She hadn't been adventurous, but she'd been active, always joining clubs and activities. He'll never know what triggered the change in her, but he worried that he carried the same trait deep inside him. He could enjoy a moment, like sharing Christine's favorite spot in the world, but he would force himself to move on.

"What I want now," he said gruffly, "is to read your infamous bucket list."

She gave a start of surprise and chuckled. "Fine, Travis I'll show you my list. But no laughing, do you understand?"

"Agreed." He didn't feel like laughing. He didn't mean to share something personal with Christine. He didn't know why he felt the need to expose his greatest fear. The one that he had struggled to overcome for years.

"I'll be right back." She got off the porch swing and headed for the door.

Travis didn't say anything as he watched her leave. He listened carefully as she walked through the small house. When he heard her climb the stairs, he knew Christine probably kept her most valuable items in her bedroom or closet.

His cell phone rang and Travis jumped at the harsh sound in the eerie silence. He grabbed it from his pocket and saw it was Aaron calling. Travis wanted to ignore the call, but he knew he owed it to his friend to stay in contact.

"Aaron?" Travis said quietly. "I can't talk right now."

"Did you find her?" his friend asked.

"Yes," Travis said. "I'm at her house and I think I know where the emerald is."

"You *think?*" Aaron gave a huff of exasperation. "The longer it's not in our possession, the more likely that I'll lose this emerald forever."

"I'm taking care of it." He glanced at the door. Christine was going to come back shortly, and he didn't want her to overhear his conversation.

"Why don't you just confront her?"

"I was ready to, but my instincts…"

"Instincts?" Aaron repeated. "Forget your instincts. Let's just go with my plan and call the cops."

"No." He knew getting the police involved was the best option, but he didn't want to do that to Christine. She'd grabbed the emerald on a whim or out of opportunity. Undoubtedly, she had no idea what it was worth. "You will have your lucky charm back by the end of the week. I promise."

"I don't like this, Travis. How do we know she's not working for Hoffmann? He left immediately after the game. That emerald could be long gone."

Travis looked around Christine's porch and front lawn. "I can honestly say that she's not an internationally wanted jewel thief." He heard Christine walk down the stairs. "I have to go. I'll call you when I know more."

"Travis!" Aaron said.

Travis disconnected the call and turned off his phone, not wanting any more interruptions. He slid the phone back into his pocket as Christine stepped onto the porch. She held a sheaf of papers that were yellowed and wrinkled with age.

"Here you go. I'm not sure what you're going to find in this list," Christine said with a hint of uncertainty. She thrust it toward him and he accepted it. He glanced at the faded print and knew she was trusting him with something deeply personal.

"Are you kidding?" he said as he gestured her to sit next to him on the creaky porch swing. "In this list is our next adventure."

THE STORM SWEPT IN later that night. Christine leaned against the column of her front porch and watched the jagged fork of lightning in the dark sky. She heard the patter of rain on the roof tiles and felt a sprinkle of raindrops on her skin. She was protected from the ferocious and wild elements but she yearned for a closer look.

She'd survived having Travis look at her list of dreams. He didn't laugh or roll his eyes at some of the fanciful items. He wanted to know the reasons behind the goal and what had the greatest meaning to her. He understood what drove her and she felt Travis knew her better than anyone.

"I should have known you'd like storms."

Christine froze when she heard Travis's voice right behind her. She refused to follow the urge to look at him. "Do you like them?" she asked.

"Always have." He was standing close, his chest grazing her back. "When I was younger, I wanted to harness the lightning. Never figured out how to do it."

"We don't get storms around here too often." Christine rubbed her bare arms to ward off the sudden chill. "It's usually peaceful and quiet."

"You should make the most of the lightning," he whispered in her ear, making Christine shiver.

"I am not running outside," she said over the crack of thunder. "Knowing my luck, I'd get hurt."

Travis rested his hands on her shoulders as the lightning flashed, illuminating the sky. "Have you ever made love in the rain?"

"No." *Don't even think about it. What he's suggesting is forbidden.* Christine pressed her lips together as the thoughts swirled around her mind. She shouldn't consider the possibility. Someone would see them and she would have to take care of the mess long after Travis left town.

"Have you chased a storm?" Travis asked.

The roar of thunder matched the thrill coursing through her veins. She shouldn't make love to Travis again. She could fall fast and hard for this man and he wasn't looking for any kind of commitment. But she might never have another chance to experience the magic they shared.

"There are many things I haven't done," she said as she rested her hand on the porch column. "I want to stand in the eye of the storm, but I'm staying here."

"Why?"

"Because I can have a taste of danger." She finally turned

around and looked at him. She saw the stark need in his eyes and knew it mirrored her own. "And still stay in my comfort zone."

He rested his hand on the column, taking away any chance for her to escape. "Why do you want to stay on the sidelines?"

"The risks outweigh the rewards," she said. Right now she felt as powerful as the storm that whipped around them, but she knew she was vulnerable and insignificant. "I need to look after myself. No one else will."

"I can take care of you," he said as he met her gaze.

She closed her eyes, wishing she could ignore his words. She knew he could protect her while making her feel wildly alive. Travis could make her want things she didn't think were possible. "You don't know me. You don't know what I need."

"I know you better than you think," he said as he rested his forehead against hers. "You follow the rules, but you still don't get what you want. It doesn't matter how much research you do or how many baby steps you take. You're not making your dreams come true. What you need to do is plunge headfirst into trouble. You'd be surprised how much fun the unknown can be."

What he was suggesting sounded terrifying. "You don't know how miserable it is to reach for the stars and fall flat on your face."

"It's not as painful as letting a dream go," he continued. "You let a few dreams slip past your fingers because you couldn't see the possibilities. Everyone told you that it couldn't happen. I'm here to tell you that you need to take a leap of faith."

Christine squeezed her eyes shut as the lightning lit up the night sky. Travis saw more than she realized. She didn't like feeling this exposed.

"Forget the rules," he said. "Forget your surroundings. Just follow your instincts."

She tilted her head to the side and opened her eyes. Travis

was standing a kiss away from her. "What do your instincts tell you?" she asked in a throaty voice.

"That you are trouble. I have no self-preservation when it comes to you," he admitted. "I want you no matter what the consequences and that should scare the hell out of me."

"I already know how this is going to end," she declared as her heart raced.

"Liar," he said with a hint of a smile. "You don't know what I'm going to do. What I'm willing to risk. And that scares you because you don't know what's going to happen next. Well, I'll give you a hint. It includes you and me naked on this porch."

She gasped as the image flickered in her mind. It was daring, risky and forbidden. She knew better than to consider it, but the idea was unbearably exciting. "Let me be clear," she said in a whisper. "We are not having sex on my front porch. Someone might see us."

"I won't let that happen," he promised with a growl. "What happens tonight is for my eyes only."

Travis reached out and threaded his hands in her long hair. She thought about twisting out of his hold—they might get caught, they might be exposed—but she welcomed the shadows, wanting to hide how she felt.

She didn't understand it, couldn't control it. Yet she also couldn't see Travis's expression. Was there a gleam of lust or triumph in his eyes? The porch was too dark, but she felt the tension in him. She grabbed the front of his shirt and pulled him forward. Travis went willingly and their mouths collided.

The kiss was hot, hard and hungry. Excitement swirled inside her, wanting to break free. Christine slid her hands under his shirt, enjoying the warm skin and solid muscle beneath her fingertips.

Travis skimmed his hands under her thin blouse. Her stomach muscles clenched; his hands were large and she shivered as he tugged her blouse over her head.

The lightning forked across the night sky, illuminating them for a brief moment. She saw Travis's face. His features were drawn, intense. He lowered his head and pressed his mouth against the curve of her neck as he slid her bra straps down her arms.

He unhooked her bra with ease and curved his fingers in the center between her breasts. Her pulse fluttered as he rubbed his knuckles against her sternum. With the flick of his wrist, the bra fell away.

Her breasts felt full and heavy under his gaze. Her nipples were tight and aching for his touch. She gasped when Travis covered her breast with his hand. Unease trickled down her spine. His touch was possessive. But she didn't want to be claimed. If he claimed her, she would never let go. Christine didn't want to think about the future. She only wanted to focus on this moment. For tonight, Travis was hers.

Pushing all thoughts away, Christine held Travis's face and covered his mouth with hers, pouring everything into the kiss. She stopped only when she felt as though her lungs would burst.

Christine wrestled with his shirt until she dragged it off his arms. Her movements were urgent and eager, but she didn't care. This was a second chance to be with Travis and she needed to capture a lifetime in one night. Christine pressed her chest against his, moaning with pleasure as skin met skin.

The thunder crashed over them, but she barely heard it as Travis gathered her in his arms and lowered her onto the padded bench behind them. The pillow was soft and cool against her flushed skin.

Lightning flashed as he teased her breasts with his mouth. The light and shadows danced along them as she rocked with Travis. It was as if this wasn't real but part of a fantasy world.

Travis kissed and licked a trail down her stomach. His mouth was gentle and soft, but his hands were strong and

demanding. She arched as he drew her jeans from her hips
and pushed them aside.

She was naked, reaching for him, and he settled between
her thighs. Travis bent his head, kissing her passionately,
relentlessly. Christine groaned, frantic now as the pleasure
rushed through her. She wanted to hold on, was determined to
bring him closer. But Travis was in charge, bringing her to the
edge with a devilish flick of his tongue before she climaxed.

She was still trembling with the aftershocks as he pulled
away. Christine's bliss knew no bounds and then she saw
Travis unzip his jeans. She was mesmerized by his swift and
elegant movements as he put on a condom before he settled
again between her legs.

Desire gripped her body as the tip of his erection pressed
against her heat. Thunder bellowed. Travis paused for a split
second before he surged forward. She rolled her hips to meet
his thrust. A crack of lightning blazed across the sky. This
time she wanted the brightness. She wanted to see Travis at
his most elemental.

"Hold on to me now, Christine," he said through clenched
teeth.

She clung to him in every sense. His thrusts were powerful and it wasn't long before a climax erupted from deep inside her. She arched into Travis, her cries swallowed by the
roar of the storm.

Christine held on tightly as Travis's movements grew
wilder. She didn't want to let go. And she wouldn't until tomorrow. Tomorrow she would return to her quiet life. Tonight
she would make memories.

CHAPTER ELEVEN

TRAVIS SLOWLY SAT UP in bed and looked around Christine's room. The sun was just beginning to rise and light streamed through the window shades. He was reluctant to look for the emerald. This might be his only chance to search, but it felt wrong.

He looked at Christine as she slept next to him. He was beginning to believe she hadn't taken the emerald. He thought she was the only one who had the opportunity, but he didn't have hard proof. Did he immediately decide she was the one because it gave him a chance to follow her? Had he just been fooling himself so he could see her again?

No, he wouldn't do that to Aaron. This emerald was important to his friend and it was worth a lot of money. Aaron wasn't a millionaire, but he took care of his large and extended family. The winnings and that emerald made a big difference to his family's future. Travis had failed Aaron and he had to make it up to him. He wouldn't have pursued Christine unless he truly believed she had stolen the gem. He couldn't afford to second-guess his instincts and he wasn't going to be distracted by her again.

Travis rose from the bed and looked at the shelf across the room. There were a few decorative boxes. She could have placed the gem in one of those.

"What time is it?" Christine asked sleepily.

He froze when he heard her voice. "It's still early. Go back to sleep."

Christine slowly sat up and pulled the sheet around her naked body. She yawned and flipped her long hair from her face. "Where are you going?"

"I was going to sneak back into the bed-and-breakfast," he lied.

There was a beat of silence. "Oh, okay."

Travis could tell from her tone that she didn't believe his answer. "Where did you think I was going?" he asked as he walked back to the bed.

"I don't know. The first thought that crossed my mind was that you were leaving. Leaving town."

He was surprised that her mind had jumped to that conclusion. "Do you want me to leave?"

"No," she admitted as she glanced out the window. "But I know that Cedar Valley is too small for you. Too quiet."

It was the quiet that had woken him up before dawn. He had avoided silence for as long as he could remember. "I've been to smaller places."

"I would love to hear all about it," she said as she watched him crawl back into bed. "What do you think of Cedar Valley?"

"It reminds me a lot of you," he said as he tugged the bed-sheet from her hand.

"Really?" She tilted her head back as if she didn't know if she should take it as a compliment. "How?"

"It has a natural beauty," he said softly. "It's caring and nurturing."

"Sometimes too caring," she whispered.

He didn't know if Christine was talking about Cedar Valley or herself. "And after a while, you can't imagine being anywhere else."

Her lips twisted with bitterness. "Don't worry, the feeling doesn't last."

Travis frowned as his slow, sweet seduction took an unexpected turn. "What do you mean?"

"My dad lived here all his life and when he was having financial problems, he just got up and left. Never heard from him again. I assume he found a more exciting life." She turned her head away. "My mom left when she got remarried. She couldn't wait to get out of here."

"And you stayed behind."

"More like got left behind. I hate feeling like that. I think I get a little too attached to people because of it." She sighed and made a face. "Not to scare you or anything, but I had considered staying in Vegas for one more day. It didn't feel right to leave."

Travis stared at her. If she had stayed one more day she might not have gotten away with the emerald. "Why did you leave?"

"Because everything was perfect. I didn't want to mess things up by staying. It was my first one-night stand, and I didn't want to get it wrong."

He smiled at her confession. "Your first, huh? Why wasn't that on your bucket list? Or do you have a separate one for sex?"

"A bucket list for sex?" Christine laughed and shook her head. "I can barely get through the one I have now."

"What would be on that bucket list?" His body hardened as he thought about Christine's fantasies. Would they be sweet and romantic or would they shock him? "What is the one fantasy that you want to do more than anything else?"

The light in her eyes flared. Travis knew he was the star of that fantasy. He felt humbled and powerful at the same time.

"What is it?" he asked hoarsely.

"I want to let go. Lose control." Her voice was barely a whisper. "I don't want to think or worry. I just want to feel. Be swept away."

"I have an idea," he said quietly as a sense of urgency pulsed inside him. He could give her that. He could make her fantasy come true right now. "But I don't know if we're ready for it."

She licked her lips. "Tell me."

Travis leaned closer to Christine. This could change everything between them. She'd probably say no and he'd never be invited back into her bed. Yet he was compelled to suggest it. Travis knew this might be what she was looking for—and he wanted to be the one to do it for her.

"Let me blindfold you."

CHRISTINE HESITATED. SHE'D never been blindfolded. Had never been able to relinquish control. The idea of making herself vulnerable excited and scared her.

"Why?" she asked. She trusted Travis. Had shared her bed, her body, but this was different. She wished she wasn't hesitating. Travis was strong but tender. He would take care of her and her needs. Only he would be able to watch her and she wouldn't get to see the lust in his eyes or watch him become overwhelmed with pleasure.

"I won't do anything you don't want to do," he promised softly as he grabbed the pillow he slept on and removed the pillowcase. "But you'll experience total freedom."

She wanted to know what that felt like. But to receive freedom, she had to give Travis freedom over her. Was she ready for that?

Yes. Christine wanted to explore this with Travis. She couldn't imagine doing it with anyone else. "Okay," she finally agreed.

Excitement shone in Travis's eyes as he folded the white pillowcase. Christine's heart beat against her chest as he covered her eyes with the cotton. The sudden darkness surprised her. She automatically put a hand on the blindfold and stopped. She didn't need to test it. She could pull it off at any time.

Christine cautiously reached out to touch Travis. Her fingertips clawed at the air. Where was he? She knew he was still on the bed; the mattress hadn't dipped. Christine tilted her head and listened. She heard his uneven breath.

"Travis?" she whispered.

Christine jumped when she felt his mouth brush against the curve of her throat. The sensation was gentle and yet she felt exposed.

Maybe she wasn't ready for this. She liked to know what was going to happen. She needed to predict, to plan. It was what she did best.

Travis pressed on her shoulders and lowered her onto the bed. Christine tried to slow her pounding heart. She lay before Travis naked but she didn't feel the need to flaunt her body or pose seductively. She was tempted to drag the bedsheet to her chin, but what she really wanted was to see the desire in his eyes. Watch him moan in appreciation.

He held her face with his large hands before slipping his tongue past her parted lips. She felt the stubble on his chin rasp her skin. His fingers shook as he contained the wild energy that whipped through him.

Christine skimmed her hands through his hair. It was softer than she remembered. She touched his face, memorizing the lines, as Travis explored her. He was both demanding and lovingly tender. His kisses would shift from playful to daring. She could no longer assume what he would do next.

She gave up trying and the freedom she felt was shocking. All she had to do was feel. Enjoy. Travis showed her how much he desired her, how much she aroused him. Christine wanted to savor the pleasure that rushed through her veins. The excitement swelled inside her.

"Travis," she whispered as she squeezed her eyes shut. She arched back as he covered her nipple with his lips and drew her into his mouth. She moaned as the fierce tug went straight to her core.

Travis cupped her sex and she bucked against his hand.

She stretched against the bed as the lust scorched her from head to toe. Christine murmured with approval, rocking her hips as he teased her.

Suddenly, he withdrew. Christine frowned and bit her lip. She felt alone. Cold. She swayed her hips but he wasn't there. She didn't feel him or hear him. The mattress moved as he left.

But he wouldn't leave her. Christine's stomach twisted. Travis wouldn't play games. He wouldn't abuse her trust. She didn't know why she believed that. He made no promises but it didn't need to be said. She knew.

Her curiosity was too much. She squeezed the bedsheet when she really wanted to push the blindfold from her eyes. "Travis?"

"I'm here," he said, his voice thick and husky. The relief seeped through her when she heard the rip of foil and realized he had paused only to put on protection.

Christine waited impatiently for his return. She needed his touch. She wanted to be surrounded by him. She wanted to think of nothing but Travis.

The dip of the bed warned her. She felt Travis's hands on her knees as he settled between her thighs. She wrapped her legs around his hips tightly and put her hands on his lean, muscular body. She adored the feel of his power and strength when her fingers trailed down his back.

Christine's fingertips dug into his skin when she felt Travis against her entrance. She barely realized Travis's hands were under her hips before he entered her with one stroke.

Her gasp echoed in her ears as Travis remained still. Now, more than ever, Christine wanted to see him. She needed to see the straining tendons in his neck as he struggled to make this moment last. She wanted to see him surrender before she heard his hoarse cry of release.

Travis's even thrusts drove her wild, and she didn't want to hide her primal responses. The pleasure built higher and higher. Their mingled breaths. The musky scent. She was intensely aware of the tension and subtle changes in his body.

She couldn't fight it any longer. Christine surrendered to the sensations. To Travis. The climax flashed hot and bright. Travis groaned as her pulsating body triggered his release. With one final thrust, Travis tumbled on top of her.

Christine wrapped her arms around him. He was heavy and warm against her. She didn't want to move. Christine was panting as she pushed the blindfold away with a shaky hand. "Travis?" she murmured.

"Mmm?" He didn't lift his head but instead nestled his face against her throat.

"The next item on my sex bucket list is for *you* to wear the blindfold."

His chuckle vibrated against the crook of her neck. "Now I *really* want to see this bucket list."

LATER THAT MORNING, Christine stepped into Jill's Dry Cleaning on her way to work. Her kitten heels clicked on the floor as she strode to the counter. "Good morning, Jill."

Jill glanced up from her computer and her eyes widened. "And good morning to you, Christine. Is that a new dress?"

"No," Christine said as she adjusted the belt of her pink wrap dress. "I don't usually wear it because the fabric clings and the neckline dips low." She wasn't sure what had possessed her to wear it today. She had been drawn to the feminine lines and the pretty color. And when Travis saw her in the dress, his eyes lit up just as she knew they would.

"Looks great," Jill said with a knowing smile. "Especially when you wear your hair like that."

"Thank you." Christine absently reached for the clip at the top of her head. She had swept part of her hair up and allowed the rest to tumble past her shoulders. She should have scooped it up in a tight braid, but for some reason she couldn't be bothered.

"Are you here to pick up?" Jill asked. "Because I don't have your clothes ready yet."

Christine waved the question aside. "No, no. I'm in no rush. I'm here because I have a question." She rested her arms on the counter and met Jill's curious gaze. "Do you have a bucket list for sex?"

Jill's mouth dropped. "Say what?"

"Seriously. I don't have a sexy bucket list. I have a regular bucket list with one hundred items but not one entry has to do with sex. What do you think that says about me?" Christine asked and bit her bottom lip with worry. "Maybe Darrell was right."

"Darrell is an idiot," Jill replied. "You didn't have a sexy bucket list when you were with him because you didn't trust him with your fantasies. And when you date someone like Darrell it's no surprise."

"You can't blame it all on him." Although she would love to, especially after he announced to the whole world that she was boring in bed. And there was some truth to that. She hadn't been as bold and daring with Darrell as she was with Travis.

It should have been the other way around. She had known Darrell forever and had dated him for years. Why did she feel closer to Travis? Shouldn't she be more cautious with a man she'd just met?

"I'm twenty-eight years old and I never gave much thought to my sexual fantasies," Christine confessed. "Do you have a sexy bucket list?"

"I did. I completed it."

Christine jerked her head up. "Seriously? Does everybody have one but me?"

"It was a short list," Jill said matter-of-factly. "Why all the questions?"

Christine stood up straight and smiled with pride. "You

are looking at someone who just put together her bucket list for sex this morning."

Jill propped her chin on her fist. "Congratulations. Anything crossed off?"

Christine felt her face heat. "A few things, actually." She wasn't going to go into detail. Jill was her friend, but her list included her most private fantasies. The only person she wanted seeing it was Travis.

Jill wagged her eyebrows. "Did Travis show you his bucket list?"

"No…" He didn't hint at any of his sex fantasies. She felt there was an uneven exchange: she had revealed more than she'd planned, and he hadn't shared much about himself. "I didn't ask."

"Why not?" Jill asked. "That's not like you at all. You are always asking people about their goals and dreams. Why not ask about your lover's sex fantasies?"

"I don't want to find out that I can't fulfill his deepest wish," Christine said quietly. "What if my bucket list doesn't look like his? What if it turns out I'm not enough for him?"

Jill pursed her lips as she considered Christine's fears. "I don't think you have anything to worry about. He's here because of you."

His pursuit had surprised her and she guessed it showed the depths of his feelings. "He's not here to stay."

"Perfect!" Jill exclaimed. "You're not looking for a relationship."

"That's true…" This was supposed to be temporary. She needed to remember that.

"And you've said yourself that you let opportunities slip by. Now is the time to grab the chance to be with him before he goes."

"You're right. You're right." She lifted her hands as she thought about what her friend said. "I know you're right."

"Where is he now?"

"Asleep." Christine tried to hide her naughty smile. "In my bed."

Jill's eyes widened. "Is that so? You're not worried what the town will think?"

She shrugged. "I dated Darrell for years and no one was scandalized."

"That's because Darrell isn't a sexy stranger you hooked up with in Vegas," her friend pointed out. "People are going to think you're on a wild ride and you're heading for a fall. They just hope you're not going to do it with their money."

"I've never given them any concern in the past." Christine glanced at her watch and started to walk to the exit. "And Cedar Valley will realize that no man—not even someone as hot as Travis Cain—will turn my life upside down. I have everything under control."

Jill shook her head. "Famous last words."

CHAPTER TWELVE

TRAVIS PARKED HIS motorcycle in the Cedar Valley Bank's parking lot later that afternoon. He sighed as he reached for his cell phone. He did not want to make this call, but he'd put it off for the past few hours.

Aaron answered on the first ring. "Tell me you have the emerald."

Travis wished he could. He sat on his motorcycle and looked at the bank in front of him. "We have a problem."

His friend let out a long, agonizing groan. "What happened?"

Travis rubbed his hand over his face. "I don't think Christine has the emerald."

Aaron gasped. "We're too late? Did she hand it over to Hoffmann? Or has she sold it?"

"No, I don't think she had anything to do with it," Travis explained. How could he believe she was a thief? She was quiet, gentle and a terrible liar. She was so determined to focus on the rules that she wouldn't break a promise or the law.

"Why would you think that?" Aaron asked.

"I thought she was the only person who could have stolen the gem." He still remembered the hurt and pain he'd felt when he believed Christine had played him for a fool. Maybe he had been too quick to accuse her. "But obviously I was wrong."

Aaron didn't say anything for a moment. Travis imagined

his friend tearing out his long blond hair. "You said you had the emerald when you went to her hotel room."

"I thought I did." He'd been so distracted with Christine's sweet seduction. He had lowered his guard, knowing he was safe with her. "I'm almost 100 percent positive I had the emerald."

"Did anyone go into that room while you were there?" Aaron asked. He had asked the same question when Travis first told him about the missing lucky charm. "Room service? Housekeeping?"

"No." He had fallen asleep, but there had been no signs of any hotel employee entering Christine's room.

"She could have slipped it to Hoffmann's security guys while you weren't looking."

"Not possible."

"Dude, I asked you to look after the emerald because you are the only person I trust in the world other than my wife. You are street smart, you are daring and I've trusted you with my life so many times."

"I'm going to make this right."

"And you still think this woman is innocent?"

"Yes," Travis replied. He couldn't explain to Aaron that he trusted his gut instinct on this. Aaron, the most understanding guy he knew, simply wouldn't understand.

There was a tense moment of silence. "You slept with her again, didn't you?" Aaron said accusingly.

"What?"

"Yeah, that's what I thought. What kind of pull does this woman have? It's bad enough that you fell for her innocent routine the first time. I thought you went there to confront her. Instead you went there to have sex with her. Again."

Travis had to admit that his actions looked bad.

"You were so sure she was the one who had the emerald," Aaron said. "And the minute you see her, you suddenly think there is no possible way she could have played you."

"That's not it at all. I looked through her house." He hated every minute of invading her privacy, but he had been thorough. When he didn't find the gem with her valuables upstairs, he systematically went through every room in Christine's house after she'd left for work. "There is no emerald. No jewelry at all. No valuables, no money and no indication that she knew who to sell it to."

"Keep looking," Aaron urged. "I know she has it. She must have it hidden somewhere else. Try her workplace. Try her purse. Hell, try *her pocket*."

"My gut tells me she never had it." If she had taken it from him, Christine would never have allowed him to get close to her, to stay in her house alone and to sleep next to her.

"Then who does?" Aaron's voice rose, and Travis pulled the phone away from his ear. "We have lost three days looking for my lucky charm. It could be anywhere."

"My guess is Pitts and Underwood," Travis said as he got off his motorcycle and walked to the bank. "They were determined. They could have pickpocketed me after Christine won her jackpot."

"You would have noticed."

Travis thought he would. He had learned how to avoid getting pickpocketed during his travels. He knew how to steer clear of certain situations. But all his experience meant nothing when his full attention had been on Christine. "I'm coming back to Vegas and we can figure out our next move."

"You sound disappointed," Aaron said. "I thought you'd be thrilled to get out of Cedar Valley."

He didn't want to leave. It shocked him, scared him, but he couldn't shake the feeling that he wanted to stay. How could he leave Christine after this morning? Her trust in him had been a rare gift. What was she going to think if he left now? It was the worst timing.

"I don't know what you hope to accomplish in Vegas," Aaron asked. "All my poker buddies have left Nevada. Hoffmann and his crew are gone. The trail grew cold while you were chasing Christine. And it's too late to go to hotel security or the police."

Travis gripped his cell phone more tightly. "I'm not giving up," he said through clenched teeth. "I'm going to find the emerald."

"I thought having you carry the emerald in your pocket was a stroke of genius," Aaron said. "I saw this emerald broker from Colombia do it. He had been dressed casually and had no security following him. Everyone was focused on the guy in the expensive suit and his bodyguard. No one knew the other guy had the gem."

Travis had heard that story several times in the past few days. He closed his eyes as he gathered the last of his patience. "I don't know what went wrong."

"When are you coming back?" Aaron asked. "I can't stay in Vegas for much longer or Dana will start asking questions."

Travis halted at the bank's entrance. "She doesn't know the emerald is missing?" That surprised him. He thought Aaron told his wife everything.

"I don't want her to worry," Aaron said defensively. "That emerald isn't just my lucky charm. It is the most expensive thing I own and I was going to use it for…" Aaron's voice trailed off. "If that's gone, I don't know what I'm going to do."

Travis didn't think he could feel worse about letting his friend down. "I'm going to leave Cedar Valley in an hour," he told Aaron.

"Fine. I still think Christine took the emerald. She's the only one who got close enough to it," Aaron said. "She was the only one who had the chance to swipe it while you were sleeping."

"Christine doesn't have it," Travis insisted. She didn't have any of the telltale signs that a person demonstrated when they were hiding something. "I have to go and tell her I'm leaving."

"She doesn't deserve the courtesy," Aaron said. "But keep me posted."

His friend ended the call abruptly. Travis stared at his cell phone before putting it into his pocket. He should have known babysitting a jewel was too easy. The guilt he felt was overwhelming. Aaron had trusted him and now he would never forgive him.

Travis stepped into the bank and scanned the area. There were no customers. He waved at Laurie at the teller window and looked for Christine. He saw her sitting in her office talking on the phone.

He paused as he watched Christine. She looked happy and relaxed. Beautiful and radiant. She was smiling as she listened to the caller. It was a different smile than the one she gave him. When she looked at him, he felt special. He felt connected to Christine. After a lifetime of being alone, he wasn't ready to walk away from her.

"Travis?" Harold, the portly security guard, interrupted his thoughts. Travis turned and saw Harold beckon him with the curl of his finger. "I want a word with you."

Travis shoved his hands into his leather jacket and strolled toward the older man. "Why do I have the feeling that I'm in trouble?" he asked with a smile.

Harold did not return the smile. His eyes narrowed as he gave Travis a hard stare. "You may not be used to living in a small town, but you need to be careful."

Travis went still. "What are you saying?" Did Harold overhear his phone conversation? Did he know there had been another reason for following Christine to Cedar Valley?

Harold looked around and lowered his voice. "You were at Christine's house last night. And this morning."

Busted. He knew he had pushed his luck. He should have returned to the bed-and-breakfast before dawn, but he found a sleepy and satisfied Christine irresistible. He had to curl Christine against him. He hadn't meant to fall back to sleep.

He was going to have to bluff his way through this. He didn't understand small-town etiquette but he was pretty sure he'd just made life a little complicated for Christine. "And?" Travis asked.

Harold held Travis's gaze. "Your bed was untouched at the bed-and-breakfast."

"How do you know that?" Travis looked around. The citizens of Cedar Valley were better at spying than he gave them credit for.

"Listen, we're happy that Christine has found someone," Harold said. "But information is power in Cedar Valley. Someone could give this relationship a slant and Christine would have a fight on her hands."

"Why would anyone care?" Travis's voice rose and he immediately snapped his mouth closed. He took a deep breath. "We are talking about two single adults in the privacy of someone's home." Well, there was that moment on the porch.

"City guys. They just don't get it." Harold shook his head and leaned forward. "When a young woman sows some wild oats, the ex-boyfriends stir up trouble."

"Darrell." The guy looked weak but he was the kind of man who would hold a grudge. "What is he saying?"

"That she had a hidden wild streak that's out of control," Harold said. "And when a bank manager taps into her wild side, people get nervous and they check their bank statements a little more closely."

"I got it, Harold. Thanks for explaining it." It was for the best that he was leaving now so he could protect the reputation she'd worked so hard to build. "I'll make sure Christine doesn't get in trouble because of something I did."

CHRISTINE HUNG UP the phone and automatically glanced at the door of the bank. Excitement fizzed inside her when she saw Travis chatting with Harold. When she rose from her seat, she felt almost dizzy with joy.

Oh, no. Christine pressed her lips together but the smile broke free. She was falling hard for Travis Cain.

She had to hit the brakes on these feelings. She wasn't looking for a relationship. She wasn't going to get distracted by a guy when she needed to focus on her goals.

Christine saw Faye Lamb and her daughter, Bonnie, enter the bank and walk past Travis. She frowned and looked at the calendar on her desk. It wasn't Monday. Christine walked out of her office and flashed a big smile at Travis before she approached the two women.

"Good afternoon, Mrs. Lamb," Christine greeted her most valuable client as she gingerly shook the older woman's hand. "Hello, Bonnie. I didn't expect to see you today."

Bonnie gave her a weary smile. "My mother can't make up her mind on which piece of jewelry she wants my brother to have."

"I've decided that I should divide it evenly between the children," Faye announced.

Christine gave a quick look at Bonnie, who shrugged. It was as if she was tired of the fight. Christine didn't know why Faye was making these decisions, but she knew it wasn't her place to say so. "Let me get Laurie to help you with the safe-deposit box."

As she patiently went through the same routine, Christine had a strong sense of déjà vu. Faye wore a black dress and discussed the story behind the pink cameo brooch. Bonnie, dressed in a T-shirt, yoga pants and a baseball cap, looked through her bag for the safe-deposit key. Christine wondered how many times they went through this ritual and how many times they would go through it again.

She felt a sense of relief as Faye and Bonnie went to the safe-deposit boxes with Laurie. Christine hurriedly returned to her office and found Travis waiting for her. She wanted to touch him. Greet him with a kiss. Instead, she kept her hands firmly at her sides and stood next to him.

"Travis? What are you doing here?" she asked. She tried to play it cool, but she knew she couldn't hide her emotions. When Travis was around, the air was electric. The colors were brighter and she felt the anticipation beat in her chest.

Travis looked away. "I... Is there somewhere more private where we can talk?"

Her smile froze. There was something in the tone of his voice that warned her she wasn't going to like what he had to say. "Is something wrong?"

Travis swallowed roughly. "I have to leave town."

"Oh." The news felt like a slap. He was leaving? After what happened this morning? What they shared had meant something to her. It wasn't to experiment or try something different. She'd explored her most secret fantasy with Travis. But it was just a bit of fun for him. "I understand."

"No, I don't think you do." He reached for her hand, but she yanked it away. She couldn't let him touch her. Not when it meant so much to her and so little to him. "A friend of mine needs my help," Travis explained. "He had this emerald and someone stole it."

Christine rolled her eyes. A likely story. "You could do better than that. Just tell me the truth. You're ready to move on."

"Christine, I'm not making this up," he insisted as he watched her closely.

"Okay, fine." She didn't believe a word he said. She'd heard it before. *We'll keep in touch. It's only temporary. It's not you, it's me.* "Are you planning to come back?"

"I don't know how long this is going to take."

She noticed he'd sidestepped the question. He wasn't coming back. She had given herself to this man and he was ready to go. She only had herself to blame. She knew this had been a fling. Her feelings, however, were stronger and more intense than any she'd felt in her other long-term relationships. "When are you leaving?" she asked, hating how her voice cracked.

"In an hour," he said apologetically.

She pressed her lips together. She didn't get another night with him. Christine knew she shouldn't be greedy. She got more than she had ever hoped. She should be grateful but she wasn't. She felt as if something special had been ripped from her hands. "I'm sorry you have to go."

"I am, too."

She looked away and saw Faye and Bonnie walking back to the exit. "Could you excuse me for a second? I need to check on a customer."

"I'll be right here."

But only for a little while, Christine reminded herself as she walked out of her office. Travis was leaving. There was nothing here to tempt him to stay.

Christine dabbed her fingertip against the corner of her eye. She would not cry. She was not going to cause a scene. She'd been through this before. One would think breaking up would get easier.

She knew she wasn't exciting enough for someone like Travis. He had been looking for her alter ego in Vegas and got the Cedar Valley version instead. She'd opened up and shown him her dreams and fears. She'd pushed past her comfort zone, but it still wasn't enough to intrigue Travis. He couldn't get away fast enough.

"Was there anything else you needed, Mrs. Lamb?" Christine asked hoarsely.

"No, we just needed to pick up one thing," Bonnie said. She gave Christine a curious look. "Are you feeling all right, sweetheart?"

"I'm fine, thank you for asking," Christine lied. She wondered what she looked like. Were the tears shimmering in her eyes? Was her face blotchy as she tried to keep her emotions in check? Right now she felt as though the light inside her had been snuffed out without warning.

"Is that man from Vegas keeping you up all night?" Faye

asked. She looked past Christine and waved at Travis, who stood in the doorway of her office.

Bonnie's face turned bright red. "Mom!"

"I remember what it was like with my sweet Stanley," Faye said with a wistful smile. "Sometimes he bought me jewelry after an especially wild night."

Bonnie groaned with embarrassment and clapped her hand over her eyes. "Mom, I don't think Christine wants the details. I certainly don't."

"I don't think I've heard these stories," Christine teased, although she wasn't sure if she wanted to know about them. Right now hearing stories about another person's love life was like pouring salt on an open wound. "What did he give you? Have you shown me those pieces of jewelry?"

"Maybe I should show them to your man," Faye said with a wink. "Give him a few ideas."

"Okay, Mom." Bonnie decided to intervene. She placed her hand on her mother's back and directed her to the door. "You got the brooch you wanted. We need to leave now if we want to make it to your dentist's appointment. Sorry, Christine."

"No need to apologize. Her stories are the highlight of my day," Christine said. She smiled and felt her bottom lip tremble. Travis wasn't her man. He wouldn't commemorate their wild night with a memento because it didn't mean anything to him.

Christine watched the women leave. She was reluctant to return to her office. To Travis. She wasn't ready to say goodbye.

Faye shuffled to a stop and raised her hand. "Bonnie. Where is my bracelet?"

"On your wrist, Mom."

"No, see." She waved her hand and the stack of bracelets jingled. "Where is the gold chain one?"

"It's right..." Bonnie's voice faded. She stopped and looked at the floor. "Where did it go?"

Faye turned around. The worry lined her forehead as her eyes clouded with confusion. "I was just wearing it a moment ago."

Bonnie held out her hands as she scanned the floor. "Nobody move."

Christine saw Harold walk over to them but Travis was already at her side. "Is there a problem?" he asked Bonnie.

"My mother's gold bracelet is missing."

Christine sensed the tension in Travis's body. She didn't need to look at him to feel his gaze on her. "Really?" he said in a strange tone.

"Travis, this is not your concern," she said as she started to retrace the path Faye and Bonnie took. "I know you have to leave."

"Change of plans, Christine," he said as he walked alongside her. "I think I'm needed here."

CHAPTER THIRTEEN

"I'LL GO CHECK OUTSIDE, Mrs. Lamb," one of the tellers offered as she hurried through the glass doors. "Maybe it fell off on your way here."

"I'll go check around the safe-deposit box," Bonnie said.

Travis watched the women spread out in different directions, but he stayed with Christine. It couldn't be coincidence that an emerald and a piece of jewelry were missing when she was around. Travis glanced at Christine as she looked around the marble floor. She seemed genuinely concerned.

And when he had mentioned the emerald to Christine, there had been no sign of guilt or discomfort. She wasn't trying to hide anything. Instead she had rolled her eyes at his explanation. Either she was a very good actress or she had no knowledge of the emerald whatsoever.

He'd stopped believing she had stolen the emerald and he would have defended her honor to Aaron. But he couldn't ignore that Faye Lamb's bracelet was missing. Did Christine have something to do with the stolen item?

Travis walked over to the older woman. She was pacing while wringing her hands. "When was the last time you saw the bracelet, Mrs. Lamb?"

"Call me Faye," the older woman said with a flirtatious smile. She patted her graying hair and gave him a thorough look.

"I'm Travis," he introduced himself and gently took her offered hand. The woman liked her jewelry. She wore several rings on each hand. There was a diamond-encrusted watch on her left wrist and a stack of bracelets on her right. She wore a gray pearl necklace that he hadn't noticed at first because it was almost hidden by her high-neck black dress. Matching pearl earrings peeked out from under her hair.

"I like to switch up my jewelry. My husband gave me a little bauble for special occasions or milestones. But I always wear this bracelet." She rubbed her fingers along her wrist. "I rarely take it off because it has a tricky clasp."

"What does it look like?" The bracelets she wore were an eclectic mix of styles and metals.

"Well…" Faye pursed her lips as she thought about it. "It's like a chain."

"It's a knitted gold design," Christine said as she approached them. "It is like a chain but with the volume turned up. It's made from yellow gold and it was created by a famous French jeweler in the late sixties."

"How do you know so much about the bracelet?" He hated being suspicious of Christine but it sounded as if she had been researching the piece of jewelry.

"Faye told me all about it. Her husband gave it to her when they found out she was pregnant with her first child. The chain is supposed to symbolize how the child will link them together forever."

Travis noticed how Christine's expression softened as she told the story. He should have known she was a secret romantic. Unfortunately, he was terrible at gift giving. He would never be able to give a thoughtful present like that.

"The clasp was loose," Faye said. "I was going to have the jeweler fix it before I gave it to Todd."

"It's not there," Bonnie said as she hurried back into the room. "I didn't see anything."

"I remember! I had it when I walked in," Faye said. "The light hit the gold just so. And then Christine came to meet us."

And that was the last Faye saw of it, Travis silently added.

He looked at Christine and wondered where she could have put it. She had gone back to her office. There could have been plenty of places she slipped the bracelet without it being detected.

"Do you remember seeing it?" Travis asked Christine.

She shook her head. "I wasn't really looking," she said as she crossed her arms. "I saw it yesterday. We were talking about it."

"Oh, that bracelet was special to me," Faye said as she started wringing her hands again. "I can't believe I lost it."

"We're going to keep looking," Christine promised.

Harold tapped Christine on the shoulder. "We should call the police."

"Do you really think that's necessary?" Christine asked. "I'm sure it will turn up."

"Considering how much Mrs. Lamb's jewelry costs, yes."

Christine's shoulders sagged with defeat. "You're right, Harold. Please call them."

"Oh, no, no, no." Faye waved her hands to stop the security guard. "I don't want to cause any trouble."

"I'm sure we'll find it," Bonnie said.

"The bracelet is important to you and it's worth a lot of money," Christine said. "We should follow procedure. Why don't you sit down and wait?"

"Let me get you some coffee," Laurie volunteered as she guided Faye and Bonnie to the chairs next to the coffee machine.

"When was the last time you had to follow this procedure?" Travis asked.

"It hasn't happened before." She gave Travis a sharp look. "Why?"

He shrugged. "I wondered about its success rate. Do you think she was wearing the bracelet?"

"Yes." Christine's reply was instant. "She wore it every day."

"Do you think she forgot and took it off? Does she display any signs of forgetfulness?" Travis asked. There could be a logical explanation for the missing bracelet. Christine may not have any part in this.

"No, she's in good health. She has a routine and that seems to help her. Bonnie also lives with her. If there were any signs of deterioration, she would know."

"You said today was a change of routine."

"Mrs. Lamb comes in on Monday," Christine explained. "She goes to the safe-deposit box, where she keeps her jewelry because she's uncomfortable keeping it at home. This afternoon, she said she changed her mind about the jewelry she was giving to her son, Todd."

"Does she frequently give her jewelry to her children? Maybe she already sent it to Todd." He didn't know why he was determined to find a reasonable explanation. It was important to him that Christine had nothing to do with it.

"She hasn't had an opportunity to part with her jewelry," Christine said. "Todd doesn't visit, and Bonnie would know if her mother had mailed it."

Travis watched Faye and Bonnie as they waited for the police to arrive. They both looked upset. "What if she wasn't giving it to Todd?" Travis whispered to Christine. "What if she's selling it off?"

"It's possible that she says she's handing it to the next generation when she's really selling the pieces. But how would it help her to say it was lost?"

"Insurance money?" Travis suggested.

"She won't get anything from us," Christine said quietly. "A bank doesn't have to pay for lost items from a safe-deposit box. Mrs. Lamb would have to see if it's covered by her homeowner's insurance, but that's not always the case."

He had run out of possible scenarios. The only explanation was that the bracelet had been stolen. "I don't think it's lost," Travis murmured. "I think someone took it."

"No." Christine shook her head. "No way. I trust everyone in this bank."

"Everyone?"

She met his gaze and abruptly looked away. "Yes, even
you. You were nowhere near Faye Lamb and her daughter."

But you were, Travis thought as he watched the tension
build inside Christine when she watched the police car enter
the parking lot. *You were close enough to remove it from
Faye. And you have an unusual habit of being around when
jewels go missing.*

"JILL, IT WAS AWFUL," Christine said as she took the last sip
of her beer and looked around the bar later that evening. She
was in the corner booth with her friend and Travis, but she
felt as if she was in the harsh spotlight. She had caught the
eye of more than one person. She saw the silent accusation.
She heard the snatches of conversation.

Her neighbors believed she had something to do with the
missing bracelet.

"We can't find Mrs. Lamb's bracelet anywhere," Christine
continued. "The police took a report, and I swear I felt as if
I was being interrogated like a criminal."

Jill nodded her head. "Yeah, I heard all about it."

"I'm sure you did." She leaned back and rested her head
on Travis's arm. It felt good to have him around. She wanted
to curl into him and hold on tight. But she shouldn't get used
to the feeling. No doubt he was leaving soon and would be
long gone before the case of the missing bracelet was solved.

"I heard Laurie made a big show of opening her purse and
her desk to prove she didn't have the bracelet. And then everyone followed her lead because they didn't want to look as
if they were hiding anything." Jill rolled her eyes and took
another sip of her drink. "Who needs a search warrant when
you have Laurie around?"

It had felt strange to prove to her coworkers that she didn't

have the bracelet. Christine had always been considered trust-
worthy until today. Now the good citizens of Cedar Valley
were starting to think her wild streak included stealing.
"Maybe I'm paranoid, but I feel as if everyone has been giving me dirty looks all day."

"I'm sure it's your imagination," Travis said.

"No," Jill said matter-of-factly. "They think she had something to do with the missing bracelet."

"Why?" he asked. "There's no proof. She doesn't have a
history of stealing, does she? Why would they be quick to
suspect Christine?"

Jill gave him a pointed look.

"You have to be kidding me," Christine muttered. It was
already happening. The people of Cedar Valley didn't trust
her, didn't trust her judgment, because she was with Travis.
Worse, she didn't feel the need to hide it.

"I'm lost," Travis admitted. "What are you talking about?"

"Christine has been in Vegas recently," Jill said, checking off her list with her fingers. "Jumped out of a building.
Gambled. Hooked up with a stranger. There's no telling what
she would do next."

"These people know me," Christine insisted. "I've never
given them cause for concern."

"They thought they knew you. But you're changing. Right
before our eyes," Jill said with a proud smile.

Christine smacked her hand on the table. "I didn't take
the bracelet."

"I know that," her friend assured her. "Travis knows that.
Let the dust settle and everyone will say they knew it, too."

She shook her head. "What if they don't find the bracelet?"
The possibility made her sick. "People are going to blame me.
They aren't going to trust me or trust the bank."

"They'll find the bracelet," Travis said.

Christine wasn't so sure. They'd searched the bank and she
had a bad feeling that someone she worked with had stolen

the bracelet. One of her coworkers was going to let her take the fall. The idea made her stomach churn. "I need to leave," she said as she grabbed her purse. "I'm sorry."

"Don't worry about it," Jill said. "Get some sleep. Things will look better tomorrow."

Christine seriously doubted it, but she forced a smile. "Thanks, Jill."

"And it was good meeting you, Travis," her friend said as Travis got up and helped Christine out of the booth. "Drop by my store anytime for a chat."

Travis nodded and walked alongside Christine. He had his hand on the small of her back as he escorted her to the door. No one blocked her exit with Travis at her side. He made her feel safe and protected. If only he could make this whole mess go away.

"I've never been accused of anything like this before," Christine said as they walked down the block to her home. "The people of Cedar Valley know me. How else would I have become bank manager?"

"This is my fault," Travis said quietly. "My being here is causing a dent in your reputation."

She glanced at him. The sidewalk was dark with a lone streetlamp, but she could tell the responsibility he felt weighed heavily on him. His head was bent and his shoulders hunched as he shoved his fists into his jacket pockets.

"I refuse to believe that," she declared. "Someone is going to find that bracelet and everyone will feel guilty for blaming me. But tomorrow it's going to be so hard to walk into the bank."

"Then skip it," Travis suggested. "Take the day off."

Christine's eyes widened. That was the last thing she should do. "I can't miss work. I already had a three-day weekend."

"I'm sure you have plenty of sick days. Use one of those."

"The day after there was a missing piece of jewelry in

the bank? Which most people think I'm responsible for? If I miss work, everyone will automatically think I'm guilty."

"And if you go into work, you will have to deal with curious and angry customers. The bank is going to be a three-ring circus. That's more reason for us to leave Cedar Valley for the day."

Christine couldn't shake the feeling that Travis wanted to escape Cedar Valley more than she did. He seemed restless and uneasy since he had walked into the bank earlier today.

"What would you like to do?" he asked. "I think we can find something on that bucket list of yours."

"Travis, no." She stopped walking. "I can't leave. Especially not now."

"This is the perfect time," he argued. "Aren't you feeling as if you're under a microscope? That everyone is watching you?"

"Are you?" she countered.

"Yes."

She shouldn't have been surprised by his blunt answer. Travis obviously felt small-town living too confining. "What do you usually do when you feel this way?"

"I find another challenge. An adventure. There has to be something around here that we can do. It might take up a day or two."

"Travis, I'm going to stay. I don't expect you to." Her throat tightened as she spoke. She didn't want him to leave, but she knew she couldn't keep him here. "You were already planning to leave before the bracelet went missing."

He crossed his arms. "I said I'm staying here."

"You say it as if it's some form of punishment." After what he'd said about his childhood, she understood his need to keep moving. Travis didn't want to settle down and risk being like his grandmother. "I'm sorry that Cedar Valley isn't exciting enough for you."

He sighed. "That's not true."

Christine started walking again. "Oh, and that whole story about how your friend lost an emerald? You need to come up with a better excuse."

"I don't have to make excuses," Travis said as he followed her. "If I want to go somewhere, I do it. If I want to try something, I do it. I don't let anything hold me back."

She knew that was a pointed reference to her. How she had dreams and plans but it was all talk and no action. "Then why are you still here?" She stumbled to a halt as a horrible thought occurred to her. "Do you think I took the bracelet?"

He paused. Travis opened and closed his mouth before looking away.

She reared back as if she'd been slapped. The man she trusted, the man with whom she had risked her reputation, didn't trust her. "You're taking quite a while to answer," she said brokenly.

"I don't think you took the bracelet," he finally said.

"You don't sound convinced," she said tiredly as the fight went out of her. At least her friend believed in her. "Good night, Travis."

"Good night, Christine," he called to her. "Sweet dreams."

"Send me a postcard," she said as she walked up the steps to her house. She immediately regretted the suggestion. She didn't want to be reminded of what she thought she had with Travis. Of what it could have been.

"I'm not leaving," he said. "I'll be at the bed-and-breakfast."

"Why?" she asked as she reached for her keys. "You don't want to be here."

"You have no idea what I want," he said in a growl.

She opened the door and turned. Christine saw him standing on the sidewalk. His stance indicated he was ready to defend himself, but she knew he wanted to get away.

"You don't have to say a word," she said as she leaned on the doorframe. "I see it in your eyes. The way you were pacing in the bank. The way you couldn't sit still at the bar. I've seen it before. You're going stir-crazy and want to leave."

"Try not to compare me with your father."

"Point taken." Maybe some of the pain that was pressing against her was from the memory of her father's desertion when the going got tough. "Travis, I don't want to be the one holding you back," she said as she stepped inside her house and started to close the front door. "Do what you want, but I choose to stay."

CHAPTER FOURTEEN

CHRISTINE STARED BLANKLY at her computer screen as she slumped into her office chair. She felt as if she had trudged through the day with no energy or interest. The gray day had leached out all color and the quiet had been overwhelming. She wanted to bolt out of the bank and run back home.

But she couldn't. She *wouldn't*. She would get through this. She always did. When her dad disappeared and left her with a financial mess to clean up, she had kept her head down and worked hard. When Darrell broke up with her in the most public fashion, she went through each day as if nothing had happened. She would regain control of her emotions when she followed her routine. The disappointment and pain would eventually morph into a stupor.

Only she didn't want to be numb anymore. She wanted the blood-pumping and heart-racing moments. The hard kisses and the soft caresses. The moments before she took a risk, uncertain of the outcome, were the scariest. But they were better than the numbness. Travis had showed her that.

Travis. Christine closed her eyes as her chest clenched with regret. She would never see Travis Cain again. She should have kept her mouth shut. He was trying to help and could have shown her a good time. A chance to forget and feel free.

But he had been wrong and there was a difference between taking a calculated risk and avoiding a problem. She had to show up at work and face the curious and concerned customers. Christine opened her eyes and looked around the bank, which had been a hub of activity all day.

She knew how Cedar Valley operated. The quirks, the unwritten rules and the rituals. Travis didn't need to. He had no intention of staying in Cedar Valley for long.

She could picture him here. He wouldn't blend in, but the people would gravitate to him. Christine let out a staggered sigh. She'd never know. He'd probably already left. She hadn't seen or heard from him since she'd rejected his offer to take the day off. Christine squeezed her eyes shut as the tears burned in the back of her eyes. She had been holding him back. The man was on his way to some grand adventure while she stayed home.

She glanced at the main lobby of the bank. Would it really have been the end of the world if she had taken up Travis's offer? There had been no emergency, no urgent matter. If she had gone with Travis, she could have done something fun and exciting. Made memories. Sure, some people would have seen her absence as proof of guilt, but she knew she wasn't in the wrong.

She heard the entrance door of the bank open. Christine's breath hitched in her throat as she turned to see who arrived. Her shoulders sagged with disappointment when she saw Darrell stride through the door.

Christine watched as he walked past Harold. Darrell was so different from Travis. Darrell was the golden boy while Travis had a dangerous edge. Her ex had a selfish side that he hid behind a charming smile. Travis had been considerate in and out of bed. Darrell had made her feel lacking; Travis showed her she was everything she wanted to be if she just took a chance.

Darrell was walking toward her office, and Christine swallowed a groan. He was the last person she wanted to see. Her emotions were raw and uneven. She didn't think she could be polite to her ex-boyfriend, but he was a customer. Following habit, Christine rose from her desk and walked out of her office to greet him.

"Darrell," Christine said, standing at the doorway. If she allowed him into her office, she'd never get rid of him. She clasped her hands in front of her. "How is everything going at the bookstore?"

"I'm doing great." His voice carried through the small bank. "Better than ever."

"That's good to hear." She had helped him from the moment he decided he wanted to go into business on his own. She remembered the long hours as she guided him through the paperwork and assisted him in preparing the carriage house. He had been grateful for her work and she was thrilled to see a dream become a reality.

But he wasn't willing to reciprocate and help her achieve her goals. She had wanted to travel and expand her world. Climb mountains to see if she could do it. Meet every challenge and become the daring woman she always wanted to be. Not only had Darrell claimed he was too busy with his store, but he thought her needs were a waste of time.

And he didn't know all of them. She was so glad she'd never shown Darrell her list. Sure, getting a tattoo wasn't as fulfilling as building your own business, but that goal had a reason behind it, which Darrell never asked about. Travis, on the other hand, understood that goal. He knew she wanted a permanent symbol that honored the person she was today.

"So, what can we do for you today?" Christine asked with a professional smile. It had been a long, trying day. Trust Darrell to show up when the bank was supposed to close in five minutes. He probably had a difficult problem with no easy solution, but she wasn't going to stay after business hours for him.

Darrell shoved his hands into the pockets of his pressed chinos. "Did you really meet this Travis guy in Vegas?"

Christine jerked her head and frowned. That was the last thing she expected to hear from Darrell. "Why do you ask?"

"It's okay, Christine." He reached out and cupped her shoulder in his hand. "You can tell me the truth."

She stepped away from his touch. "I don't know what this is all about." And she wasn't telling him anything. She had always held back with Darrell, and she knew that made her just as responsible for the lack of passion and intimacy in their relationship.

"You were upset about what I said—under the influence, I might add." He flattened his hand against his chest. "It wasn't my fault."

The day he apologized for his actions would be the day she'd keel over in surprise. Christine rubbed her hand over her face. "You're going to bring that up now?"

"I realize that our breakup may have sent you into a tailspin."

She crossed her arms. "I assure you it didn't." The breakup had hurt, but she'd recovered quickly. That had been a sign that their relationship had been over long before they officially ended it. His words, however, had jolted her.

Darrell's eyes narrowed as he studied her expression. "Did you really go to Vegas?"

"I did. Why?"

He shrugged. "I heard you played strip poker and joined the mile-high club."

"Excuse me?" A laugh erupted from her throat. "And you believed that? Do you know me at all?"

"I know you're mad at me and you need to prove me wrong. Did you pay Travis to come up here and pretend to be your lover?"

She raised her eyebrows. "Wow, you really *don't* know me. Darrell, you need to stop reading so much fiction."

"You have to admit—" he looked at her from head to toe "—you are not the type of girl he goes for."

Christine automatically brushed her fingers against her fake pearls as she glanced at her gray pantsuit and flat shoes. She certainly wouldn't have caught Travis's attention if she'd worn this outfit in a Vegas casino. "According to you, I'm not the type *any* guy goes for."

"There's something that just doesn't add up," Darrell insisted.

"Because he's exciting, sexy and a little bit dangerous?"

Darrell's pale face reddened. "Yes," he bit out.

Christine motioned him closer with the curl of her finger. "I'm going to let you in on a secret."

Darrell's blue eyes lightened as he leaned forward. "Yes?"

"It's none of your business," she whispered theatrically.

"He's not your boyfriend, is he?" Darrell asked as he took a step back. "That's why you won't give me an answer. You need to prove to everyone at Cedar Valley that I was wrong and you made a deal with this guy."

"I didn't make a deal with her." Travis's voice was right behind them. "And she doesn't have to tell you anything about our relationship."

"Travis." Her heart lurched when she saw him come from behind her and stand next to Darrell. She clasped her hands together to keep herself from grabbing him and holding him tight. She couldn't take her eyes off his rugged face and piercing brown eyes. "What are you doing here?"

He gestured at one of the clocks on the wall. "The bank is closing for the day and I decided to pick you up from work."

"Thank you," she said with a bright smile. The energy was pulsating through her as she met his gaze. "Travis, have you met Darrell?"

"Yes, he has," her ex-boyfriend bit out.

"I'll go get my purse," Christine told Travis. She walked to her desk when she heard Travis speaking to her ex.

"So, Darrell," he said in a soft, lethal tone that made her

pause, "do you or do you not believe that Christine has a wild streak?"

"I've never seen it."

"I bet you didn't." Travis's voice went lower. "Which makes me wonder why you're telling everyone in town that Christine's out of control and she shouldn't be trusted."

Christine's hand slipped on the drawer handle. When did Darrell say that? And how did Travis know?

Darrell nervously cleared his throat. "You're confusing me with someone else."

"No, I'm not," Travis replied with confidence. "But I'm going to settle your curiosity once and for all. She has a wild side but she's not reckless."

Darrell scoffed at his statement. "Why should I listen to you?"

"I've seen her wild side many times," Travis said. "And she will never allow herself to lose control. You know that, but you want to play mind games with her. What I can't figure out is if you're angry that she proved you a liar, or if you're angry you never saw this side of her."

"She has no sides," Darrell insisted. "I should know. I dated her for years."

"Really?" Travis drawled. "Name one thing on her bucket list."

"Her what?" Darrell asked.

"Exactly," Travis said. "She didn't trust you enough to tell you what she wanted out of life. And I don't trust you at all. Cause any more trouble for Christine and you will deal with me."

Christine quickly grabbed her purse and hurried out of her office. "I'm ready," she told Travis.

"I don't have time for this," Darrell declared. He pivoted on his heel and marched out of the bank.

Christine raised herself on her tiptoes and placed a kiss on Travis's angular jaw. "Thank you, Travis."

"You're welcome." Travis slowly turned his attention away from the main entrance and gave her an incredulous look. "That guy really thought you paid me to come here?"

She shrugged. She didn't want to point out the obvious—that someone like him would need extra incentive to notice someone like her. "He thought I was boring and you don't," she explained. "Either he's worried that he missed out on something or he can't figure out why I'm different with you."

"Why are you different with me?" Travis asked as he curled his arm around her waist and escorted her to the door.

"I'm not that different," she admitted. "I haven't done anything on my bucket list since I got back home."

"We'll have to work on that," Travis said. "I have a few ideas."

Christine and Travis said goodnight to Harold and walked out of the bank. As they strolled to the parking lot, Christine stopped, a question burning in her mind since the moment she saw him in the bank.

"Travis, why are you still here? I thought you left town."

"I was going to," Travis said quietly. "I didn't think you wanted me around and I had planned to leave immediately."

"I'm glad you didn't." She wanted him near, but knew it was only a matter of time until he left.

"But the more I thought about it, I realized that you were right." Travis sighed. "If you took the day off today, you would just be avoiding the problem. You would only face more problems the next day."

"So what have you been doing since I last saw you?"

"I've been here." He extended his arms and gestured at the downtown area. "I figured the problem is that your neighbors don't know me. So I decided to introduce myself, drop by some stores and listen to gossip. And you should hear some of the rumors. Apparently you won me in strip poker."

Christine groaned and covered her face with her hands.

"Don't worry. I set them straight," he said. "I told them it was blackjack."

"Travis." She lightly punched him in the arm.

"It's going to take them some time to get used to me," he said as he reached for her hand and laced his fingers with hers. "I'm not an expert on small towns, but I know they don't warm up to strangers quickly."

Christine's breath lodged in her chest. Was he considering staying for more than a few days? "I don't want to be the one keeping you here," she said. "I know you don't like Cedar Valley."

"I don't *hate* it," Travis said as he led her to his motorcycle. "I see the good and the bad. It doesn't offer entertainment or excitement on a silver platter. That doesn't mean it's not there. You have to look for it."

"That's true," Christine said. How often had she and her friends created a scavenger hunt or found something fun to do just out of sheer boredom? "You haven't seen my Cedar Valley."

"I guess I need a guide, Christine." His eyes sparkled and Christine recalled how he'd offered his services in Vegas. "Show me your Cedar Valley."

She pursed her lips as she pretended to think about his request. "It's going to take more than one night."

He raised an eyebrow in disbelief. "Seriously?"

"Face it, Travis. You're just not doing Cedar Valley right," Christine said. "Let me show you the way."

TRAVIS STOOD ON the rock ledge and listened to Christine as she pointed out landmarks along the mountain range. The thick forest was behind him and the scent of the trees wafted in the air as they had walked on the carpet of brown fir needles. The trail to the ledge had an eerie feel to it, but that had more to do with the ghost story Christine told than the fog nestling low between the spindly trees. They had arrived at the edge of the forest just as the sun was beginning to set.

Travis reached for Christine and held her in a loose embrace as they watched the sky turn pink and purple.

"Isn't this place gorgeous?" Christine asked in a hushed tone as the colors changed against the blue mountains. "Okay, so it's not the volcanoes in Indonesia."

"It's beautiful." It was a majestic sight. He understood why this was Christine's favorite spot in Cedar Valley. Probably her favorite spot in the world.

"Jill and I used to rock climb around here when we were younger."

He looked at Christine and saw her wistful smile. "Why did you stop?"

"We always wanted to do more, try different locations, but we never got around to it." She glanced up at the sky. "We should head back before it gets dark."

"Thanks for showing me your Cedar Valley," Travis said. He had a feeling that not many people knew about this spot.

"I'd like to show you more," she said as they followed a path back to the forest. "Maybe someday."

"*Someday* is my least favorite word," he said. "It sounds so far away and vague."

"So are your plans," she said.

That was true. His next move wasn't clear. He wanted to stay with Christine, but she was the one woman whom he shouldn't be with. Her world was small and she had difficulty finding the courage to break out of her comfort zone. She lived in the same house she grew up in and her friends were the same people she knew from kindergarten.

That may appeal to some people, but it was a warning sign to him. If he stayed in Cedar Valley, would it be like his childhood? Would he follow the same pattern as his grandmother?

"My grandmother always used the word *someday*. *Someday* she'll feel better. *Someday* she wouldn't be so afraid. But her fears ruled her life—and mine," he said as he followed Christine through the forest. "When I was out on my own,

I decided that I wouldn't get too comfortable, too set in my ways. *Someday* wasn't going to be in my vocabulary."

"You achieved your goal," Christine said as she looked over her shoulder. "You don't have a home, you're in constant motion and you didn't follow the same path as your grandmother."

Travis nodded slowly. "True, but I made those choices out of fear. I've had a lot of exciting moments in my life, but it hasn't all been a grand adventure." There had been times when he'd been weary, lonely, and he'd wondered what he had to show for his life. He wanted to create something lasting, have a circle of friends instead of acquaintances. He wanted someone to worry about him. "I want what you have in Cedar Valley."

Christine tripped on a tree root. She immediately regained her balance and turned around. "Are you sure? This town doesn't have a lot to offer."

"It has you." He felt like all his travels, all his wandering, had brought him to Christine.

She ducked her head as if his simple statement flustered her. "What are you going to do here?"

He hadn't thought that far ahead. He remembered something he had heard about Cedar Valley. "According to Darrell, this is the Pacific Northwest's premier weekend destination."

Christine made a face. "He may have exaggerated."

"I can make it better." He didn't know if his travel experience would help or if he was setting himself up for a big failure, but he was ready for the challenge. The idea, the future, excited him. But first he had to address one of his biggest failures. "I do have to leave soon to help my friend Aaron."

"The one with the emerald?" she asked, a smirk on her face.

"It's true! He had an emerald. He found it when we…" Travis winced. "You know, I'd better not tell you that story. It doesn't make me look very good."

She pressed her lips together to refrain from smiling. "There's a story that makes you look worse than the one where you lost the emerald?"

"Yes," he said. "There are a lot of unflattering stories about me. I have had so many injuries and bad luck when I was going after something. But I hope to make up for it when I find the emerald. I lost Aaron's lucky charm and I have to help him."

"I understand," she said as she continued making her way through the forest. "You need to fix it or you'll never forgive yourself."

"But there is one thing I want to take care of in Cedar Valley before I leave."

Christine paused in midstep. "What's that?"

"I'm going to clear your name," he said as a protective instinct welled up inside him. "I'm going to find out what happened to Faye Lamb's bracelet."

Christine turned. "How are you going to do that?"

He had no idea, but he had to do something. "Just wait and see."

She smiled. "You don't have a plan, do you?"

"Christine, you should know by now that I never have a plan."

CHAPTER FIFTEEN

"TRAVIS, WE'VE GONE through this a hundred times," Christine complained the next morning as they sat on the porch swing drinking coffee. She was swaddled in her pristine white bathrobe while Travis only wore jeans. She didn't want to discuss the theft anymore but she knew Travis would not be distracted. "None of our theories make sense. We have no idea who took the bracelet."

"What does your gut instinct tell you?" he asked as he looked out onto the street.

That we won't get to the bottom of this case and should leave it to the experts. "I don't think it was any of my coworkers. It may be that I'm too close to them, but I don't think they had the opportunity. Who do you think did it?"

"I agree," he said. "It had to be Faye or Bonnie."

"They have no motive," she felt compelled to point out again.

Travis took a sip of his coffee. Christine knew he was deep in thought. The lines in his forehead deepened and he clenched his jaw.

"What can you tell me about the Lamb family?" he finally asked.

"Not much. They have been comfortably wealthy since I can remember." Her family didn't really socialize with the Lambs. "Todd and Bonnie are at least twenty years older than me, so I don't really know them."

He tilted his head as he continued to watch the empty street. "What's the gossip about them?"

Christine took a sip of coffee and spluttered. "You want to gossip?"

"Gossip has its place, especially in small-town living," he admitted with great reluctance. "Let's say Laurie sees Harold doing something dishonest. She would want to warn others. Some of the talk is to discuss how a person did something wrong, but Laurie also wants to save people from getting caught in a dishonest deal with Harold."

"Not all gossip is correct. Remember the rumor that I won you in strip poker?"

Travis glanced at her and smiled. "That's not on your bucket list?"

She made a face. "That's not even on my sexy bucket list."

"Maybe not now, but I'm sure with very little convincing…"

Christine gave him a warning look. "Back to the Lamb family."

"Right." He returned his attention to the quiet street. "What gossip have you heard about them?"

"I haven't heard anything bad about Faye or Bonnie." She tried to remember what the townspeople had said about the Lambs. "Faye is generally well liked and admired because of her philanthropy. Most people in town are impressed with Bonnie's devotion to her mother."

"And Todd?" Travis asked.

"Todd had been in a lot of trouble when he grew up around here. I remember my parents and their friends talking about him. He was caught vandalizing, trespassing, and I think he did some petty stealing."

"And what is he like now?"

"I don't know. I guess he grew out of it because if there had been any legal trouble, we would have heard about it," Christine said. "He lives on the other side of the country and he doesn't come around very often. Only when he needs cash, according to gossip."

Travis frowned and looked at Christine. "And Faye is going to give him family heirlooms?"

"I know. I don't understand it, either," she said. "Faye only has complimentary things to say about her son. I think she believes what she wants to believe."

"What does Bonnie think?"

Christine shrugged and took another sip of her coffee. "As far as I can tell, she has no opinion."

"No opinion?" he repeated. "If we are judging Faye's choices, you can bet Bonnie has an opinion. She may not show it when they are in public, but I'm sure she has tried to influence her mother's decision. What was her expression when they told you Faye's plans?"

Christine tilted her head back as she tried to remember that day. "She didn't have one. She looked tired, that's all."

The harsh lines in Travis's face softened as his mouth tilted in a lopsided smile. "She did it."

Christine gave a husky chuckle. "Because she looked tired?"

"Sure. She was exhausted trying to convince her mother. She knew she was defeated and she decided that she'd take the bracelet."

"That's speculation," she warned him. "You have no proof."

"Think about it," he said as he set down his coffee cup and turned to face her, gesturing with his hands as he explained his theory. "Todd goes off and does his own thing while Bonnie stays behind to take care of her mom. She must be furious that Faye is splitting the jewelry down the middle."

"Let's say you're right and Bonnie wanted the jewelry for herself," Christine said carefully. "Why would she choose to take it at the bank? Bonnie didn't have to steal the jewelry in a public place. She could do that without anyone watching in her own home."

Travis exhaled sharply. "Okay, that does put a dent in my theory, but she did it. I know it." He glanced at his watch. "Where is she?"

Christine looked at the street and then back at Travis. "Are you expecting Bonnie?"

"I saw her jogging along here yesterday morning." Travis reached for her coffee cup and set it down before he helped her off the porch swing. "Come on."

"What are we doing?" she asked as he led her out the porch door. "Can I at least change? I'm still in my bathrobe."

"No time," he said as he fixed his sight on the street. "We're going to confront Bonnie."

"What?" Her legs locked and she pulled back on Travis's hand. She wanted to stop him, but he was much stronger than she was. Her bare feet slid along the wet grass. "Are you kidding me?"

"No," Travis said as he dragged her to the edge of the sidewalk. He looked down the street to see if Bonnie was coming. "She has the bracelet. We're going to get it from her."

"We have no proof," Christine whispered fiercely as she tried to pull him back in the direction of the house. "What if we're wrong?"

"She'll be angry," he predicted calmly as he glanced at his watch again. "She will probably hold a grudge and move her accounts to a different bank."

"Oh, is that all?" Christine tossed her hands in the air. "Her family is very powerful here. It would make my life difficult. *Our* life difficult," she corrected.

"But what if we're right?"

Christine thrust her fingers in her hair as panic and worry swirled inside her chest. "Yes, what if we're right and we can't do anything about it? We tip her off and she gets rid of the bracelet."

"That's why we're using the element of surprise."

She crossed her arms and started to pace around in circles. Her feet were wet and cold, but she didn't care. "Do you think this is going to work?"

He looked at her and shrugged. "I say we have a fifty-fifty chance."

"Nope. Not good enough." She shook her head vigorously. "We're not doing this."

Travis cupped his hands on her shoulders and peered into her eyes. "Come on, Christine. The bracelet hasn't been found. We need to take a risk or it will never be recovered."

Christine tried to think of another tactic. Nothing came to mind. She growled with frustration. "I'm not sure about this."

Travis looked down the street and dropped his hands from Christine's shoulders. "There's Bonnie."

Christine saw the older woman in a black baseball cap, hot-pink T-shirt and black workout pants. Her shoes were black with hot-pink shoelaces. Christine curled her toes into the wet grass and fear flowed through her veins. She grabbed Travis's arm. "Let's reconsider this."

"Don't worry, Christine," he said as he watched Bonnie get closer. "I'll do the talking."

"What will I do?" she muttered. "Interpretive dance?"

"Good morning, Bonnie," Travis said as the older woman walked past.

"Morning," she said breathlessly as her ponytail swayed from side to side. Christine noticed Bonnie didn't make eye contact. She pumped her arms without missing a beat.

Travis watched her take a few more steps. "We know you have the bracelet."

Christine winced as the panic wrapped tightly around her chest. Bonnie halted and the ponytail fell limp. Her arms went still, but she didn't drop them to her sides. She slowly turned around. Bonnie stared at them with her mouth sagged open.

This is bad, this is really bad, Christine thought. She

closed her eyes and wished the ground would open up and swallow her whole. *I'm so getting fired.*

"How did you know?" Bonnie asked.

TRAVIS PAUSED. HE WAS used to thinking on his feet. That was part of the fun, not knowing what would happen next. But it was different this time. What he said or did would affect Christine. He couldn't make a mistake. Too much was riding on his response.

"Do not say *lucky guess,*" Christine said in a hiss.

He almost regretted approaching Bonnie when he had nothing to back up his accusation. But she had confessed to it. He had to make sure she didn't take back those words. Travis decided to sidestep the question. "Why'd you do it, Bonnie? Did you need the money?"

"No!" The older woman looked hurt and offended that he would suggest that. "I would never sell Mom's bracelet."

"You took the bracelet to keep it safe," Christine said, her voice rising as she realized the woman's motive.

Bonnie glanced at Christine. "Exactly. My mom got it into her head that she wants to give all this jewelry to Todd." Bonnie shook her head and sighed. "But Todd doesn't care about the bracelet. He has no emotional connection to it. He's just going to sell it."

"Your mother has to know that's a possibility," Travis said.

"No, she doesn't. The jewelry that she wants to give Todd has to do with some milestone about him so she thinks they are just as important to him as they are to her. My mom doesn't wear the jewelry because of its value or its style. They are symbols of my dad's love."

"That bracelet costs thousands of dollars," Christine pointed out.

"So what?" Bonnie replied. "Don't you have mementos? Something that holds a special memory? Some of those pieces are inexpensive, but they are important to my mother.

She wouldn't understand why another person wouldn't value them."

"Do you plan to hide her other jewelry?" Travis asked.

"None of this was planned!" Bonnie insisted. She crossed her arms and looked away. "I didn't realize the bracelet was missing until Mom noticed. I went back to our safe-deposit box and saw it on the floor. The clasp was broken."

"You're in that room every week so you're very familiar with it," Christine said. "You know we don't have security cameras where customers open their safe-deposit boxes. This was your chance."

Bonnie gave a sharp nod. "I was going to hold it until Todd's visit was over. You have to believe me. Once he was gone I just thought I would 'discover' it in a drawer or something."

Travis wasn't sure if he should believe Bonnie. From what he'd seen and heard, the woman was protective of her mother. But perhaps she had been stealing all along and this was just the first time she'd been caught. The woman managed to smuggle the bracelet out after the bank had been searched.

"How did you get it out of the bank?" he asked. "You showed everyone the contents of your purse."

Bonnie lowered her gaze and shifted uncomfortably on her feet. She lifted her hand and tapped her baseball cap.

"Under your cap," Christine murmured. "That was quick thinking. No one thought about that because we always see you with a baseball cap on."

Bonnie readjusted the bill of her cap and pulled at her ponytail. "Unfortunately, when I returned from the safe-deposit box area, Harold said to call the police." She shuddered from the memory. "I was stuck. It's not as if I could take off my cap and say, *Gee, how did that get in here?*"

Travis clenched his jaw and glared at Bonnie. "Instead you were going to keep quiet and let Christine take the fall."

"I didn't mean to do that!" Bonnie looked at Christine and

clasped her hands together as if she were praying. "The police didn't consider you a suspect. They acted like it was a low priority, as if it was all a misunderstanding and Mom probably lost it earlier that day. I was so surprised when everyone in town decided you had something to do with the missing bracelet. Christine, I never thought that would happen."

"It did happen," Travis said in growl, "and she needs her name cleared."

"I feel bad about this. I really do. I got you in trouble. My mom is upset that she lost something important to her. I got myself in this situation and I couldn't find a way out." Bonnie hunched her shoulders. "So what are you guys going to do?"

"Christine?" He glanced at her. She looked adorable in her oversize bathrobe and with a stern expression on her beautiful face. "It's up to you."

Christine was silent for a moment. She exhaled sharply and slid her hands into her hair. "Okay, this is what's going to happen. Bonnie, after your run today, you will 'discover' the bracelet in your home."

Bonnie nodded in agreement. "I can do that. I want this over and done with. I didn't sleep at all last night."

"Are you sure you want to do it this way, Christine?" Travis asked. He wasn't surprised that she would give Bonnie a way out. She didn't always follow the rules, but he didn't want Christine to find herself in the same situation.

"I do. But we have got to make it convincing," Christine said. "The last thing you want is for your mother to become suspicious of you. I know you did this to take care of her but she may not see it that way."

"You're right," Bonnie said quietly. "She would be hurt. And once I tell her I found it, I'll call the police and let them know it was all a false alarm."

"And you're sorry for the inconvenience," Christine added. "You could have sworn your mother was wearing the bracelet at the bank."

"That's it?" Bonnie asked. She looked at Travis and Christine as she took a step back. "That's all you want me to do? Are you sure about this?"

"Yeah, I'm sure," Christine said. "And I'm sorry that you'll find it before your brother arrives."

"Why are you apologizing to her?" Travis asked. "You didn't do anything wrong."

"And I'm sorry you got caught up in this," Bonnie said as she took a few more steps away from them as if she couldn't wait to get away.

"I'll see you on Monday." Christine gave a wave to Bonnie. "Business as usual."

"Thank you," Bonnie said with relief. She hurriedly turned around and sped down the sidewalk as if she was being pursued.

Travis waited until Bonnie turned the corner before he looked at Christine. "Why did you let her off the hook?"

"I went with my instincts," she said as she walked back to the porch door. "She tried to protect her mother but made a mistake. I don't think she's going to repeat it."

"See what happens when you take a risk?" he asked with a smile.

She groaned. "That was horrible! I was so nervous I thought was going to pass out. We are so lucky that Bonnie's guilt was eating away at her."

"Horrible?" he asked as he followed her. "You did great. You figured out why she did it and when. You bluff very well."

"Thanks, I think."

"Bluffing is a very important life skill," he said as they stepped onto the porch. "Especially when you're in Vegas."

Vegas. Travis bent his head as he remembered the other problem he had to fix. He had to leave Christine and he wasn't ready.

She looked disappointed and was trying to hide it. "You need to go help your friend."

"I'm coming back," he promised. "Once I find the emerald, nothing is going to keep me away."

"You don't have to convince me," she said with a wobbly smile. "I believe you. You've never lied to me or had an ulterior motive."

Travis kept silent. She didn't know that he'd suspected she had taken the emerald. *And she never will.*

"If you say you're going to return, you're going to return," she said confidently. "And I'll be here when you get back."

CHAPTER SIXTEEN

AN HOUR LATER, Travis walked into the small kitchen as he pulled on his T-shirt. Christine almost sighed with disappointment as the soft cotton covered his well-defined chest and hid the way his jeans rode low on his hips.

He frowned when he noticed Christine was still in her bathrobe. "Shouldn't you get ready for work?"

"I called in sick a couple of minutes ago," she said. "I told Laurie it was a twenty-four-hour bug."

"You did? And she believed you?"

She smiled. "No." She didn't care what her coworkers thought. She didn't know how long Travis would be gone and she wanted to make the most of the time they had together.

"Are you sure that's a good idea?" he asked as he set his hands on his hips. "You just had a three-day weekend and people still think you had something to do with Faye's missing bracelet."

"The police called me while you were in the shower. Guess what?" she asked in a hushed, confident whisper. "The bracelet was found in the Lamb residence."

"Imagine that."

She rested her hip against the kitchen table. "I updated Laurie when I called in sick. She is so relieved."

"And the rest of Cedar Valley will find out in the next ten minutes," he predicted.

"But I can't celebrate the good news with my coworkers,"

she said as she flattened her hand against his chest. "I am staying in bed for the day."

His eyebrow rose. "*All* day?"

"That's right." Anticipation beat hard against her chest. "But before I go back to bed, there's something I need to know."

Travis swiped his tongue along his lips as he stared at her mouth. "Okay, what?"

"What's on *your* bucket list for sex?"

Something wicked flashed in his eyes. "I don't have one."

She gave him a look of disbelief. "I'm sure you have some fantasies."

"I do," he said in a drawl as his intense gaze made her blush.

Why wasn't he telling her a few of them? Did he think she wasn't ready for them? Was he worried that he'd shock her? "Are there any you want to share with me?"

"Yes."

Her skin stung as her pulse skipped hard. "Name one thing on your bucket list."

"You."

She gave him a wide smile and brushed a light kiss on his mouth. "Good answer. But what's on your list?"

"You," he repeated as he placed his hands on her hips. "You are my list."

She must have misheard. "I don't understand."

"I want to make love to you outdoors. Have sex in the shower with you. Under the stars and when I first wake up. I want to make love to you slow, and I want it hard and fast. I want you and only you," he confessed gruffly. "You are my list."

"Oh," she said weakly.

"I will never get enough of you."

She believed him. His words were like a pledge. A vow.

"Tell me more," she said. "No, better yet, show me."

Christine perched on the edge of the kitchen table and parted her legs, drawing him closer. Travis cupped her face with his large hands and tilted her head up to receive his mouth. He caressed her lips with the sweetest kisses. She opened her mouth and drew him in.

Christine dipped her hands under his shirt and her fingers skimmed his washboard abs. She flattened her palm against his chest and felt his steady heartbeat under her touch.

She loved this man. Christine knew it was too soon, too fast, but she couldn't deny it any longer. The knowledge didn't scare her. She was ready to risk anything to protect this feeling, to make it grow stronger.

And she didn't want to hide her feelings from Travis. There was no longer a need. She wanted him to know how she felt about him. That she trusted him with her life, her body and her heart.

"Did your bucket list include stolen moments in the kitchen?" she asked against his mouth as she teased his flat nipple.

"Yes," he growled, and his fingers found her hips. "My imagination about you is limitless."

She reached for her belt and untied the loose knot. She broke the kiss and met Travis's gaze as she peeled the thick cotton robe from her shoulders. The cool air wafted against her bare skin. She shivered as she watched Travis's jaw clench.

She wasn't nervous about baring herself to him. With the way he looked at her, she felt beautiful. Strong and feminine. The glint in his eyes encouraged her to be brazen.

"Touch me," she said softly, encouraging him.

He rubbed his thumb against her lips before kissing her lightly and planting more kisses on her chin and along her neck. Christine hummed her approval as he touched her everywhere, stoking her desire. It felt hypnotic; seemed otherworldly.

Christine saw his face soften as he noticed her heartbeat.

It was too loud, too fast. But this was how he made her feel. Bold and daring. She wanted to love with a roar instead of a whisper.

His hand dipped farther and Christine's breathing became choppy. He claimed her breast and she closed her eyes and bit her lip. Her tight nipple rasped against his palm. She sensed his gaze on her face and thrust her breast deeper into his hold. Christine smiled as his fingers caressed her flesh.

She lay down on the table, her fluffy bathrobe bunched up beneath her. Christine slowly opened her eyes and focused on Travis's face. Lust, raw and unapologetic, was reflected in his eyes, She heard the moan rumble in his chest.

Christine stretched her arms above her and rolled her hips. "I want your hands all over me," she murmured as she tousled her long hair with her fingers.

Travis flattened his hands on the table and leaned into her. She lifted and met him halfway for a sizzling kiss. She grasped the back of his head and dipped her tongue into his mouth. She tasted his need and his excitement. She was surrounded by his body heat and his masculine scent.

The tips of her breasts rubbed against his shirt and she grumbled with impatience. Christine reached for the hem of his shirt and struggled to remove it from him. Travis reluctantly pulled his mouth away from hers to shed the shirt before he reclaimed her with a thorough kiss.

Christine explored his body, raking her hands over his shoulders, down his broad back. He was so strong. He then dipped his head and licked her stiff nipple with the tip of his tongue.

She gasped as a delicious heat coiled deep within her. "More," she said hoarsely.

Christine felt his smile against her skin as he continued to tease her with the flick of his tongue and the edge of his teeth. She rocked under him as the wild sensations flashed through her.

Travis fondled her breasts as he kissed a path down her stomach. The tension built inside her as her skin tingled. She never wanted this feeling to end.

He parted her thighs, stroked her and covered her sex with the palm of his hand. Christine moaned as he caressed her. When his mouth replaced his fingers, Christine climaxed hard.

Sweat coated her skin as the blinding heat swept through her. Everything went silent for a moment before all her senses were reeling. "Travis!"

He continued to pleasure her as the sensations pulsed through her body. Satisfaction was hers as her fingers slackened and her legs went limp. She murmured a few words to him but her voice was weak.

Travis rose and leaned down to press his mouth against her ear. Christine shuddered when his hot breath wafted against her skin.

"What did you say?" he asked. "More?"

She swallowed roughly. "I love you," she whispered.

Christine felt the surprise course through his body. An emotion she couldn't define glowed in his dark eyes. She couldn't tell if he was going to pounce or back away.

Her muscles burned and shook as she wrapped her legs around his waist. "Don't overthink it," she said. "Go with your instincts."

Travis hesitated for a moment before he captured her mouth with his. His kiss was fierce. Emotional. Complete. And she wanted it. She wanted it all.

She encouraged him to do more. A sigh of relief staggered from her throat as he teased and massaged her body.

He broke the kiss and reached for his jeans. She saw how his hands shook as he impatiently fumbled with the foil package and then put on the condom.

Travis drew her closer to the edge of the table. Her gaze

met his and it seemed she saw everything in his eyes. The hope, the fears and the need. He was holding nothing back.

He tilted her hips and said her name when he entered her. She held on to Travis as he closed his eyes and withdrew slightly before he sank back into her heat. It was as if his body couldn't deny hers.

His rhythm was strong but unpredictable. Christine stretched out her arms and grasped the edges of the table as she met his thrusts with the roll of her hips. She lay before him, open and naked for his pleasure, but she felt powerful as Travis fought for control.

He placed his hand where they were joined and pressed against her swollen nub. Christine arched her spine as the pleasure forked like lightning. She cried out as the climax roared through her body.

She stopped moving, trying to savor the moment, and Travis went still. She felt his shudder before he thrust into her one more time. She watched his face as he found his release. It was a beautiful sight. Powerful and masculine.

Travis's groan echoed in the small kitchen. As he rested on top of her, she welcomed him into her arms. He didn't say anything as he rested his head against her breast.

She loved him, Christine thought as she closed her eyes. The timing wasn't perfect but she wanted Travis to know before he left. From now on, there was no holding back.

CHRISTINE PARKED HER car in downtown Cedar Valley. The storm clouds were rolling in, hiding the sun. A mist of rain coated the car windows as she stepped into a puddle on the sidewalk. "You're going to miss all this when you're in Vegas," she teased Travis.

"I will," he said seriously.

She smiled and kept her thoughts to herself. She had a sinking feeling that once Travis left, he would get caught up in the rhythm of Vegas, and the memory of Cedar Valley would fade under the bright lights of Sin City.

"I'm going to get a few things for my trip," he said as he walked in the direction of the general store. "Do you want anything?"

"No, but I should pick up my laundry from Jill's. I'll meet you at the car."

He raked a hand through his damp hair. "I'll be right back."

Christine watched him walk away. Travis Cain stood out in his leather jacket, jeans and boots. There was an edge to him that didn't match the cobblestone streets and Victorian houses. This town needed someone like him, but did he need a place like Cedar Valley?

Christine walked through the green double doors of Jill's Dry Cleaning. She was so lost in her thoughts that she didn't hear the chime of the bell or Jill's footsteps. Christine leaned against the old-fashioned counter and jerked in surprise when Jill waved her hand in front of her eyes.

"Are you okay?" Jill asked as she peered into Christine's face. "I heard you called in sick. I thought you were faking it so you could have one of your sex marathons with Travis. Not that I'm judging. I'm actually quite envious. Maybe I should go to Vegas and find myself a Travis."

"He's leaving today," Christine said. "I'll tell him to pick you up a guy as a souvenir."

Jill leaned on the counter. "Why is he leaving?"

"He has to go help a friend. He doesn't know how long he'll be gone."

"Huh, no time frame?" Jill asked with a frown. "I guess he stayed while you were having trouble with the missing bracelet. I heard Bonnie found it this morning. And now Travis is going."

"He'll be back," Christine insisted.

"I'm sure he will," she murmured.

She didn't like how unconvinced Jill sounded. It made

that seed of doubt in her own mind grow a little stronger. Christine straightened and flipped her damp hair over her shoulders. "Travis is in the general store right now picking up a few things. I was wondering if my laundry was done."

"Yeah." She slapped her hands on the counter and reached for a laundry basket filled with folded, colorful clothes. "I was going to call you about that."

"Is there a problem?"

She dropped the basket on the counter. "When did you start wearing men's clothes?" her friend asked.

"What are you talking about?" Christine said with a laugh. "Did you get my clothes mixed up with another customer's?"

Jill lifted a shirt from the basket. "Look familiar?"

"Oh, that's Travis's shirt." Christine bit down on her bottom lip as she remembered ripping it from his body on their last day together in Vegas. "I must have scooped it up when I grabbed my clothes on the floor."

"I think you picked up something else of his."

"Like what?"

Jill reached in the bottom of the basket and pulled out a small plastic bag. She held the edge with her fingertips. "Like this."

Christine blinked as she stared at the small green stone. The emerald caught the beam of the overhead light and twinkled. Her mouth fell open as the shock washed over her. It had to be what Travis was searching for.

"Do you think it's real?" Jill asked as she tilted her head and studied the stone.

"Yes," Christine whispered. She didn't want to think about what this meant, but the implications came crashing down on her. "Yes, it is."

"Cool!" Jill looked at her and her smile dimmed. "Isn't it?"

Christine felt hot and then cold. She squeezed her eyes shut to ward off the tears. She was such a fool. "Not really."

"Christine, what's going on?" She set down the bag. "You look like you're going to be sick."

She brushed her fingers along the emerald. "He's been looking for this."

"I would imagine."

The pain flared hot and bright inside her. "He didn't follow me to Cedar Valley because he was attracted to me," she said, struggling to get the words out. "He didn't stay because he was falling for me. All this time he was looking for this."

Jill's eyes widened in horror. "No..."

"He pretended to like me so he could get the emerald back." Christine pulled her gaze up and stared at Jill. "He didn't want me. He wanted this. It was all fake."

CHAPTER SEVENTEEN

"Christine." Jill held out her hands as if she could slow down the thoughts racing through her head. "Let's take a moment and really think about this."

"What is there to think about?" She grabbed the emerald and held it in her fist, welcoming the hard edge that bit into her palm. "It was too good to be true."

She had been stunned when Travis approached her in the casino. Thrilled but not willing to look too closely at her good fortune when she spent the weekend with him. But when he arrived in Cedar Valley, she couldn't believe he felt the strong connection between them.

No one else believed it, either. Her friends and neighbors had to see Travis for themselves. Her ex was under the impression that she'd paid Travis to play her boyfriend. Darrell was half right. It had all been pretend to Travis.

"There could be a perfectly reasonable explanation for all this," Jill said. "Just stop and think about it."

"I already know what happened," Christine said as she started to pace. There was a good explanation, but that didn't mean it was going to make her feel any better. "His friend Aaron has an emerald that he was using as collateral in a high-stakes poker game in Vegas. It's missing."

"How did you wind up with it?" Jill asked. She looked down at Travis's shirt. "Wait, did he keep the emerald in his shirt pocket? And you grabbed the shirt when you were packing. Okay, I got it now. I'm up to speed."

Christine's footsteps started to get faster. "Travis feels responsible for it because he should have kept an eye on it. The emerald winds up in my suitcase, and Travis shows up in my life. Coincidence? I don't think so."

"So he followed you thinking you stole the emerald. He didn't show up here because he couldn't live without you," Jill said as she watched Christine go in circles. "But look at it this way. He could have called the cops. He could have confronted you the moment he got in town. He didn't. Doesn't that mean anything to you?"

"It means he thought I was a criminal and he needed to do some surveillance before he pounced." And she had opened up to him because she thought he was interested. That he cared.

"What are you going to do?" Jill asked. "Tell me your plan."

Christine stopped. She felt jittery and her heart was pounding in her ears. Her mind was a jumble of emotions and instinct. "I don't have a plan. I'm just going to confront him and go from there."

"Seriously?" Jill said in a squawk. "That doesn't sound like you. You always have a plan. You analyze everything before you make a move."

Christine rolled her eyes. "When has that worked for me?"

"Okay, do you want my advice?"

She wordlessly looked at Jill.

"Keep the emerald."

Christine gasped at her friend's bold suggestion. "Tempting but no." It wasn't hers. It wasn't even Travis's. It belonged to someone who was desperately searching for it.

"Why not?" Jill complained. "Finders keepers."

Christine opened her palm and looked at the emerald. It was dark green, like the trees in Cedar Valley. Beautiful and mysterious. And a reminder that she had not been enough to capture Travis's attention. "I don't want it."

"Fine," Jill said with a deep sigh. "You have to give it to him. It's the right thing to do, I guess. And Travis returns it to his friend. Then what?"

Christine glanced out the window and saw Travis leaving the general store. His head was bent and his shoulders were hunched forward as the rain came down harder. "I don't know," she said. "He said he would come back and that he wants to be here with me. And I believed him."

"But?" Jill prompted.

"But that was before I found out about this." She held the bag out, then fisted it in her hand. "Before I realized that he had lied to me. That he had an ulterior motive to be with me."

"Then don't give him the emerald," Jill said. "Hold on to it until he's settled down here and can't imagine life without you."

"I'm not going to trap him here," Christine said, indignant. And there was no guarantee that he would fall in love with her. "If I keep the emerald, then he goes back to Vegas to look for it. The longer he stays in Vegas, the less likely it is he'll come back."

"If you give him the emerald, he may not return."

"That's a risk I have to take." She reached for the door and wrenched it open. "I have to give this to him, if only to find out the truth. Wish me luck."

Her movements felt awkward as she left Jill's. Dread twisted inside her and she found it difficult to take deep, even breaths. She wanted to believe Travis was falling for her and that he meant every word he said, but the emerald in her hand told her a different story.

She narrowed her eyes as the raindrops ran down her face. She wiped her cold skin and wished the coldness would seep into her bones and numb her. She didn't want to feel like this. Hurt and uncertain. He was going to leave in a few minutes, but she wasn't ready to take this risk. If he was here only because of the emerald, she would never see him again.

"Did you get everything you need?" she asked.

He lifted the plastic bag in his hand. "The selection is limited."

"Yeah, you get used to that after a while." But maybe he wouldn't. Cedar Valley wasn't enough for him. She wasn't enough. Even if he really meant that he wanted to be here with her, there was no guarantee he would stay.

Travis looked up at the sky and winced as the rain pelted his face. "Are you sure you don't want to come to Vegas with me? Think of the sunshine, the hot desert nights."

She was surprised by his offer. Did he really want her with him, or was he hoping she could direct him to the emerald. "I don't think I would be much use."

"You would. Look at how we found the bracelet. We make a great team. You realized why Bonnie took it and acted on it."

"Uh, that's not exactly how it happened. Your sequence is all wrong," she felt obligated to point out. "I did figure out why the bracelet was taken, and I also figured out why you really followed me home."

He frowned. "Excuse me?"

Her heart was galloping in her chest and she was tempted to back down and remain quiet. She wanted to act as though she didn't know anything, but she was tired of pretending. Christine tossed him the small bag that held the emerald and crossed her arms. "Care to explain?"

TRAVIS CAUGHT THE item out of reflex. He looked down and stared at the emerald. It took him a moment to recognize what was in his hand. And what it meant.

"You had this the whole time?" he asked roughly. He took a step back as the shock crashed through him. He'd made himself believe Christine had nothing to do with the missing jewel. He swore to Aaron that it wasn't possible and begged him not to get the authorities involved. She had played him well.

"This is why you followed me to Cedar Valley, isn't it?" Christine asked.

He glanced up and met her eyes. "I told you that I was looking for this." His voice shook with anger. She'd acted as if she had no idea what he was talking about. She'd made it sound as if she didn't believe his reasons for leaving town.

She placed her hands on her hips and glared at him. "I didn't know that you suspected I had it."

He pointed at the emerald in his hand. "And you did!" He felt betrayed. He thought Christine was a mix of heat and innocence. He didn't think she had it in her to steal from him.

She took a step forward and pointed her finger at him. "No, I didn't know I had it until just now," she corrected coldly. "I had accidentally taken a shirt of yours, and Jill found it in my laundry. She suggested I keep it."

Travis glanced at Jill's store. He saw the redhead watching from the front window. If they had kept quiet, had kept the emerald... He blanched at the thought. "Why are you telling me now?"

"I wanted the truth more."

"The truth?" He saw a movement from the corner of his eye. A few people had heard their raised voices and stepped outside to see what was going on. Christine didn't seem to notice or care.

She hesitated and clenched her hands at her sides. It was as if she was preparing for an answer she didn't want to hear. "Did you come here because you thought I stole the emerald?"

"Yes." The word was dragged from his throat. He saw the hurt flash in her brown eyes and wished he could take it back. He couldn't. It was the truth. "But I found out quickly that you didn't know about it. I thought you were the only one who could have taken it, but the more I got to know you, the more I realized you couldn't have done it."

"If that's the case, why did you stay?"

"I wanted to be with you, but I had to find the emerald."

Travis's shoulders sagged. He knew he had to tell her the rest. "I was about to leave when Faye's bracelet disappeared. Two valuables were gone when you were around..."

She tossed her hands in the air. "And despite everything you knew about me, you decided that I was some master jewel thief?"

"No," he said as he noticed an elderly gentleman in a beige trench coat holding a bright yellow umbrella slowly walking past them, not even trying to hide his curiosity. "But you have to look at it from my point of view. I thought there was a pattern."

"Why did you come up to me in the casino?" she asked. "Was it because of the emerald?"

He gritted his teeth. He didn't want to tell her. It would taint the way she looked at their relationship. "I knew you didn't have it then."

"Travis," she warned.

He sighed and raked his hands in his wet hair. "There were two men who were looking for the emerald. You noticed them at the nightclub," he reminded her. "But they had been following my friend Aaron and me all night. He'd asked me to look after the emerald. They were at the casino when I met you."

"Why did you drag me into it?" she asked.

"I needed to blend in. Make them think I was a tourist looking for a good time."

Christine's face paled. "So that's why you offered to be my guide," she whispered. "I thought it was strange that you offered your services for free."

"Hey, I never pretended to be interested in you," he said. "I was blown away when I first saw you walk into the casino. You can ask Aaron. He saw how my eyes bugged out and told me that you were way out of my league."

She rolled her eyes. "Sure he did."

"I enjoyed Vegas with you and if we didn't have two guys following us, I would have considered that the perfect weekend," he said. "I didn't want it to end. Don't you remember how I encouraged you to extend your vacation?"

"And what about the sex?" she said in a hard, cold tone. "Did you need a one-night stand to get away from those guys?"

"That night meant something to me, Christine." His throat tightened as he choked back the hurt. "What we did that night had nothing to do with the emerald."

"I'm not so sure about that." She took a step back and looked away. "I can't believe this is happening."

"Christine." He reached out for her.

She held up her hand to ward him off. "All this time I thought I had misled you. I felt guilty for pretending to be mysterious and sophisticated. But that wasn't what interested you."

"I knew you were pretending," he admitted.

She pressed her lips together and nodded. "Of course you did. You knew how to read the signs because *you* were pretending with *me*."

"Stop it," he said. "I was with you because I wanted to be with you. The real you."

"You weren't interested in me," Christine said. "You just wanted to know all about me because you thought I'd stolen your precious emerald." She stared at him, unable to hide the hurt that shimmered from her eyes. "I shared everything with you. You shared nothing with me."

"That's not true." He'd told her things he'd never admitted to anyone. She knew what drove him and what made him vulnerable.

"I used to feel half alive until I met you," she said. She flattened her hand against her chest. "You made me believe that I was exciting and sexy. That you wanted me for me."

"I do want you." He wanted to be with Christine more than anything. He was willing to risk it all if it meant building a life with her. Now it was slipping away and he was scared. He didn't know how to fix this, how to save what they had.

"You were fine sharing my bed while you were looking for the emerald," she said, her voice echoing in the quiet street. "You had sex with me to pass the time."

"That isn't what happened."

"Everyone knew something was off." She slowly turned around and gestured at the people who were watching. "I thought so, too, at first. But I didn't want to believe it. You knew what you were doing. You knew how to make me feel special and loved. You had that routine down pat."

"It was not a routine." That accusation cut like a jagged knife. "I care about you, Christine. More than this emerald."

"I kept hearing from you that I needed to let go. Take risks." She shifted her jaw to one side as she tried to contain the anger that rolled through her. "But I was the one taking the risks."

"We both were taking risks." He had been just as vulnerable as she was.

"I welcomed you into my life, into my bed," she said, refusing to listen to him. "I risked my reputation, my future, for you. I followed your lead with Bonnie because I believed you had my best interest in mind."

"You are my priority. You have been since I met you. All I want is to make you happy."

She scoffed at his statement and started walking to her car. "I listened to all the advice you gave me and it actually changed the way I view the world. You'll be very proud of me. Because I'm letting go. Of you."

"I'm coming back and we will work this out," he said as he followed her. He didn't know if he could fix this. In the past, he just moved on when a relationship crashed and burned. But this was different. "As soon as I get this damn emerald to Aaron, I'm coming back to stay."

She pulled her car door open. "Why?"

He spread his hands out. "I want to be with you."

She whirled around and glared at him. "No, you don't. It was all part of your scam."

"I didn't scam you." He bit out the words. "I wasn't truthful about why I came to Cedar Valley, but I want to stay because of you."

She leaned against the car door and gave him an appraising look, from his wet hair to his drenched boots. "Would you have approached me if it wasn't for the emerald?"

He nodded. "I like to think so."

"Even though I am everything you don't want in a woman."

Travis stared at her. "I never said that."

"You avoid standing still because you're afraid to have a comfort zone. I am firmly in mine. You're afraid that your world will get smaller and smaller. My world is about as small as it can get."

"So?"

"You knew I was trying to jump-start my life," she said. "You said you could see right through my pretense. If it hadn't been for the emerald, you would have steered clear of me."

"No, I wouldn't. I want to be there when you reach for your dreams. I admire the way you're trying to break out of your comfort zone."

"You have to admit that my life is a cautionary tale for you," she said. "But you're trying to make me believe you want to be a part of it?"

"The only thing I have to admit is that you are the best and the worst woman for me. You are the greatest challenge and the greatest adventure."

"Greatest adventure?" She gave him a look of disbelief. "How is that possible when I'm all talk and no action."

"That's not true. I see the world through your eyes. You find adventure wherever you are."

"Not true," she said as she sat down in her car. "I had a bucket list for ten years before crossing anything off. And let's not get into the one I had for sex. Or the one you supposedly had."

"My bucket list is all true."

"I was exclusively on your bucket list because you needed to get closer to me," she said in a low growl. "Did you stay in my house because you couldn't get enough of me or because you needed to search for the emerald?"

There was a beat of silence. He wanted to lie, but she already suspected the truth. "Both."

Her mouth set in a grim line as she slammed her car door closed. "You have the emerald now. There's nothing keeping you here."

"Yes, there is," he insisted. "You told me that you love me. Believe it or not, that means something to me."

"Don't let that get in your way," she said through the window as she turned on the ignition. "I'm letting go. You should do the same."

CHAPTER EIGHTEEN

CHRISTINE SAT ON her porch swing, tapping a pen against her notebook. The sun was shining and she heard the leaves rustling in the breeze. It was a quiet Sunday. Cedar Valley had been quiet since Travis left weeks ago.

She heard a knock on the porch door. "Hey, Christine," Jill said through the screen. "I thought I'd find you here."

"Come on in," Christine said. She gestured at the porch swing. "I haven't seen you in a while."

"What are you doing?" Jill asked as she sat down next to her.

Christine lifted the notebook. "I'm writing a new bucket list."

"Why?" Jill said with some concern. "What was wrong with the old one?"

She shrugged and looked down at the ideas she had scratched out on her latest list. "There were a lot of outdated dreams on that one."

"Do you really think that you are in the right frame of mind to make some life goals?" Jill asked as she leaned back on the swing. "Now isn't the time to give up on your dreams."

"I'm not giving up. I'm prioritizing," Christine explained. "I'm getting rid of the things that seemed so important when I was eighteen."

"I'm sure there are a few things that you still want to do."

"There are, but just a few. I think finding my original list upset me because I didn't achieve anything. I could have done any of those things in ten years, but I wasn't willing to take the risk."

"You were busy," Jill said.

"No one is that busy. I made excuses and I put other people's needs first. I was more comfortable helping others and was too scared to go after my dreams because I didn't want to fail. It was easier to think anything was possible if I didn't try."

"And now?"

"I thought about what I really want in life. This list represents the woman I am today."

Jill held out her hand. "Can I see?"

Christine gave her the notebook. She wasn't nervous about showing it to others. She wanted everyone to know what she planned to do. "These goals are the ones I want to achieve now. The dreams I can't wait to achieve. The ones I'm willing to risk everything to accomplish."

Jill frowned as she read the list. She turned the page and saw the blank paper beneath it. "There are only ten things."

"I pruned the list and put down the dreams I really want to pursue. Like climbing Mount Rainier." She tapped her finger on the paper. "I've always talked about that."

"I recognize a lot of these dreams. Getting a tattoo... Going to Hawaii... These are all things you've talked about in the past," Jill said as she handed the notebook to Christine. "It's a good start."

"Good start?" Christine repeated. "This is the final draft."

"But there are a few areas that you didn't mention," her friend argued. "I notice you don't have anything about falling in love or getting married. Nothing about being in a committed relationship. Is that on a different list?"

Christine dipped her head and stared at the list. "I already fell in love," she said softly. "I don't want to do it again."

"Because you're still in love with Travis," Jill said with a groan. "But that doesn't explain why you're hiding away in your house."

"I'm not!" Christine said with a scoff.

Jill's eyebrow rose as she gave Christine a knowing look. "Or are you hoping that Travis will return?"

"He won't." Christine hated how her voice hitched.

"You say that, but you've been hibernating ever since Travis left." She motioned at the pile of blankets, the stack of travel magazines and the numerous coffee cups. "That was a month ago."

"I'm not nesting or hibernating or whatever you call it. I'm taking a step back and considering my next move."

"I remember when your dad left," Jill said. "You sat on this porch for days, looking out on the street, waiting for him to come back."

Great. She'd been following the same pattern since she was eighteen. "That was different. No one kicked my dad out of the house. Travis isn't coming back because I told him to go."

Jill slanted a look at Christine. "Does he always do what you tell him?"

She chuckled at the thought. "No, but I haven't seen or heard from him since he left. I thought about calling him. In fact, I even dialed his number and heard it ring. But I didn't know what to say."

"How about, *I made a mistake. Let's talk.*"

"It's not that easy. He did have ulterior motives and I don't know if I can trust him again."

"Then you need to forget about him," Jill said as she rose from the porch swing. "You need to get out of the house and go somewhere. You don't even have to cross the city limits. Let's go to the teahouse and have a bite to eat."

Christine winced as she thought about walking around Cedar Valley. "I really caused a scene when he left. I'm embarrassed."

"Oh, please." Jill rolled her eyes. "You acted like it was business as usual when Darrell said those hurtful things."

"I had dated Darrell for a long time, but I never really opened up to him. I shared everything with Travis. He made me feel special. He made me believe that I was fun and exciting and irresistible. I liked who I was when I was with him."

"He made you feel special because he wanted to be with you," Jill said. "I saw the look on his face when he left town. He was devastated. He was hurting."

"I don't know what to think anymore, but it doesn't matter. He's forgotten all about me by now. I'm stuck here on my porch swing while he's probably in Indonesia climbing volcanoes."

"It's not fair," Jill said with a cluck of her tongue. "He started out lying to you and you were completely honest with him."

Christine bit her lip. "Okay, maybe I wasn't *completely* honest with him. I pretended to be a wilder woman when I met him. But I owned up to it."

"When you knew you couldn't keep up the lie."

Christine gave a huff of exasperation and slumped back on the porch swing. "Whose side are you on?"

"You faked it until you made it," Jill said. "You pretended to be wild with him and then you became a wilder version of yourself."

"That's because it was easy being more adventurous with him."

"Have you considered that he may have done the same with you? He acted like you were irresistible and then he discovered that you really are?"

She wanted to believe it, but her life didn't work that way. "It's possible," she muttered. "Improbable but possible."

Her friend crouched down in front of the porch swing and met her gaze. "Christine, Travis didn't make you fun and exciting. He brought that out of you because you trusted him."

"That's true."

"If you want to be fun and exciting, then you need to *do* something fun and exciting." Jill rose and clapped her hand. "It's time for another wild weekend."

Christine groaned. "That doesn't sound fun."

"That's what you said before your Vegas weekend. You listed everything that could possibly go wrong. And do you remember what happened?"

"I met Travis and got hurt. I'm still licking my wounds."

"No, you had the time of your life."

"I'm not ready," Christine announced. She knew what would happen. She would go on a trip and it would be boring. She would imagine how much fun it would have been if Travis had been with her.

"When will you be?" Jill asked as she crossed her arms. "In another ten years?"

Christine shuddered. "Good point. I'm not repeating that mistake."

Jill grabbed the notebook and pen. "Let's look at this bucket list and plan your next big weekend."

"I'm not sure about that. When I wrote this list, I imagined Travis at my side. Encouraging me. Testing me. The way he did in Vegas."

"Too bad. He did the same for you in Cedar Valley, but that's not stopping you from living here."

"I hate it when you're right." Christine held out her hand. "Give me that bucket list."

TRAVIS DROVE HIS motorcycle past the sign welcoming him to Cedar Valley. The trip had taken twice as long as it did the first time. His muscles were tight as the nervousness ate away at him. As he crossed over the cobblestone streets, he noticed that nothing had changed since he left over a month ago. He'd expected that.

The only change would be Christine Pearson. She won't

be as welcoming or as shy, Travis realized, sighing. She'd tell him exactly what was on her mind and she wouldn't hold back.

He had tried to forget her and move on. Once he'd returned the emerald to Aaron, Travis embarked on several grueling adventures. The physical exhaustion and mental fatigue did nothing to stop the flood of memories. He wasn't excited about any of the challenges. There was only one place he wanted to be.

He wanted to share his life with Christine. It didn't matter if it was in Cedar Valley or Casablanca as long as she was at his side. When he discovered that she had called his cell phone, he knew he still might have a chance. He wanted to start a new life with her, starting now.

He drove his motorcycle to the bank, waving at a few of the townspeople he recognized. One woman stared at him while she reached for her cell phone. He didn't know if she was calling Christine to warn her, but if the gossip didn't reach her fast enough, the sound of his motorcycle would signal his arrival.

This time if she hid under her desk, he was going to drag her out of there.

He parked, took off his helmet and looked at his watch. It was almost closing time, but he was sure Christine was still around. As he started walking to the bank, he saw the door swing open. His heart clenched when he saw Christine striding out.

She wore the strapless blue dress and high heels. Her brown hair was loose around her shoulders and her chin was tilted up as if she was ready to take on the world. He stopped walking as he watched her. She strode down the sidewalk with a confidence that took his breath away. Christine was as beautiful as ever, but she had changed. She wasn't holding anything back now.

He noticed the vintage mountaineering pack in her hand.

His heart plummeted. He knew what that pack symbolized. She was going on another weekend. Looking for adventure without him. Excitement. Jealousy, hot and bitter, scorched him.

"Where are you going dressed like that?" he called out.

Christine stumbled to a halt and whipped her head around. "Travis? What are you doing here?"

"I'm back." He tried to sound more confident than he felt. Her forgiveness, her acceptance, was going to make or break him.

"Why?" she asked as she slowly walked up to him. "Do you need me so you could blend into the scenery? Or did you lose something and decide I must have taken it?"

Okay, she was still upset. He should have known. "Where are you going?" he asked as his gaze traveled from the thrust of her breasts to her impossibly high heels.

She shifted her bag and held it with both hands in front of her. "On a trip."

"Vegas?" he asked hoarsely.

"No." She pressed her lips together as if she was contemplating telling him anything. "Hawaii."

Hawaii. His stomach twisted. That was worse than Vegas. He imagined her in a little bikini as a muscular surfer taught her how to ride the waves. "What do you plan to do there?"

She shrugged. "Try new things. Break out of my comfort zone. Climb a volcano."

Without him. Christine didn't need him as a guide anymore. She was doing just fine on her own. "I'm breaking out of my comfort zone, too," he said. "Here, in Cedar Valley."

"Why?" she asked. "Why here of all places?"

"This is where I want to be," he said softly. "With you."

"No, you don't," she said as the sadness flickered in her dark eyes. "You said that because you were trying to find the emerald."

"No, I said it because I meant it," he said. "I gave the emerald back to Aaron and I still feel that way. I tried to get away and forget. I've been crisscrossing the globe for the past month."

Her eyes narrowed as the corners of her mouth pinched into a firm line. "Is this supposed to make me feel sorry for you? Because it's not."

"The only thing I discovered was that all I wanted to do was be with you." He reached out and stroked his fingertips against her cheek. Hope sparked inside him when she didn't move away.

"Why? What can I offer you?"

"I love you, Christine, and it scares the hell out of me." The thought that he ruined the love she felt for him scared him even more. "I want to make plans, and you know I'm not very good at that. I'm going to try your patience and I'm going to make mistakes, but I think we're worth the risk. When we're together I feel like we're on some great adventure and I don't want it to end."

She stared at him as her chest rose and fell.

He nervously dropped his hand. "Right now I feel as if I'm on the edge of my old life. At the ledge of my comfort zone, ready to jump. And I'm ready to make the leap with you."

"I want to believe you," she whispered.

"Then give me a chance," he pleaded.

She blinked and looked at the pack in her hands.

"I understand. You're not ready to give me an answer. Fair enough." He took a step back. "Go to Hawaii and think about what I said. I'll be here when you get back," he promised.

She dropped her bag and threw her arms around his shoulders. "Why, when you can come with me?"

His knees buckled as relief and excitement clashed inside him. Travis wrapped his arms around her waist and held her tight. "So you're going to take a risk on me?"

"It's not that much of a risk," she said. "You are impul-

sive, reckless, and you have the ability to turn my life upside
down, but you are the only man for me."

"You won't regret this," he said as he bent his head to claim
a kiss. "I promise I'll give you the adventure of a lifetime."

EPILOGUE

One year later

TRAVIS SET A travel coffee mug on the bedside table. "Christine?" he said as he kissed her cheek. "It's time to get up."

Christine slowly cracked one eye open and frowned. "Travis, it's still dark outside."

"I know," he said as he helped her into a sitting position. "We need to hurry if we want to make it on time."

She pushed her long hair out of her eyes. "On time for what?"

"You'll see." He checked his watch and nervously twirled the welcome-to-Vegas keychain around his finger. The car was packed with everything they needed to have breakfast at Christine's favorite spot while they watched the sunrise. He was glad he listened to Laurie's suggestion to buy a picnic basket from the general store.

Christine tilted her head and her eyes widened as she noticed he was dressed in a raincoat, jeans and hiking boots. "Give me a hint."

"It's on my bucket list."

Her mouth tilted in a knowing smile. "I'm pretty sure we've done everything on your bucket list. Twice."

"I keep adding things," he admitted. Although this goal had been on his list for a while. Right around the same time he imagined Christine pregnant with his child. That would be years down the road, but it would be worth the wait.

This dream had also taken some planning and all of Cedar Valley had helped in one way or another. It turned out the townspeople could keep a secret if they really wanted to. "I want to make this dream happen today."

"Why today?" she asked, her voice husky from sleep.

"I can't wait anymore."

"It's Saturday, isn't it?" Christine asked as she rose from the bed. "This is your busiest day of the week."

"I got it covered." He had truly made Cedar Valley *the* Pacific Northwest weekend destination. It had been a lot of hard work, and there had been times when Christine was the only one who believed in him. Now other small towns wanted to hire him as a consultant.

"You seem pretty excited," Christine said.

"I am." He slid his hand into his jeans pocket and his fingers curled around the diamond engagement ring. He fought the urge to blurt out the proposal right now. He'd wanted to ask months ago but he'd waited until he knew Christine was ready to take the plunge. "This will be our most memorable weekend yet."

* * * * *